NO MAN FOR MURDER

No Man For Murder

Mel Ellis

j. 73040
up

HOLT, RINEHART AND WINSTON
New York   Chicago   San Francisco

BOOKS BY MEL ELLIS

I don't suppose I'll ever forget the day the judge said I would have to stand trial. From where I sat in the courtroom, I could see through a **1** window out to where a row of maple trees were red and shining in the autumn sun. I could see the courthouse lawn, still green, and the clump of purple asters around the white statue of the blindfolded woman holding the scales of justice in her hands.

It was a preliminary hearing, and I suppose I should have been listening to the judge. But I was thinking about the woman with the blindfold, and

1

how blind justice must surely be if anybody in his right mind could think of me as a killer—me, Danny Stuart, seventeen and still in high school.

I was still thinking of how ludicrous it all is, when my lawyer, Frank Benz, nudged me and told me to stand up. I stood, and the judge, Charles Hallock, looking over the top of his glasses, said, "Although the evidence is largely circumstantial, it is, nevertheless, overwhelmingly clear that Daniel Stuart *could* have killed Jacob Tabor, and there is ample evidence to indicate that the defendant might have. In the interest of justice, therefore, it is incumbent upon me to bind one Daniel Stuart over for trial on the charge of murder in the first degree."

Murder? Murder! Me? It sounded like some kind of joke, and for just one second, I felt the urge to laugh out loud.

Believe me, it was no joke . . . ! The judge was dead serious. He leaned forward—and all I could see was the shiny top of his head, bald above a fringe of gray hair—and I hardly heard his words: "The trial will be held on the first open date of the winter session of the circuit court. Although we don't normally allow for bail on a first degree murder charge, I will make an exception in this case. Bail will be set in the sum of twenty thousand dollars."

Twenty thousand dollars? Twenty thousand dollars! Why twenty thousand dollars? I wasn't going anywhere. Where would I go? I didn't want to go anywhere. All I wanted to do was to go back to the farm and get my traps ready, as I did every fall, so I could harvest the mink and muskrats along the Bloodstone River. All I wanted was to go to school, to come back to a warm home at the end of each day, to sit in the living room with the television flickering, to hear the comfortable sounds of my mother working in the kitchen.

After the judge left the bench, the court clerk took us into his office where my dad made arrangements to put the farm up as security against a twenty thousand-dollar bail bond.

As we left the courthouse, Sophia Jarrson, a neighbor who'd sometimes stayed with my two younger brothers while we were away, said she knew it was going to turn out all right and that she'd be praying for us.

I still wasn't really scared. Astounded was more like it. Amazed was probably even a better word, because all of it seemed like a dream, as though this was all happening to someone else who looked like me.

Some of my school friends were standing around the double doors when we left the hall. One of them, Mike Sturm, gave me a thumbs up, but mostly, they all just watched in silence.

On the day I had been arrested, it had seemed so utterly ridiculous I laughed about it. Even as the days went by, I thought: soon they'll catch the real murderer and then I'll be free. But it didn't happen, and the web of evidence they were spinning around me got stronger.

What really brought home the seriousness of it all was the way my mother took it. One day, she was bustling around the house cooking, dusting, sewing, mopping, and singing softly to herself, and then the next day, there she was, quiet with her hands in her lap, sitting in the shadowy alcove back of the big potted fern. She had fixed supper for us, but said she couldn't eat. I could see her from the kitchen, and I remember wondering why I had never noticed the lines on her small face or the gray hairs sweeping back from her temples. I remember thinking, too, about how blue her eyes were and how they used to shine, but how, now, they seemed dull and lifeless.

I remember Dad putting his hand on her shoulder and saying, "You just can't sit here, Martha . . . You just can't sit here." She would only sigh, and my dad would shake his head and walk slowly away.

I could have gone back to school, of course. My dad left it up to me. We were out in the kitchen trying to eat, when he said, "Danny, you don't have to go back to school if you don't want to. It's up to you." Then he looked away from my face, down at his big hands—which were so clever about fixing so many things—as though he was ashamed he hadn't made the decision for me.

4

"I think I'll stay home," I said.

"May be best," he agreed, lifting one of his hands and running the fingers through his short, curly, reddish hair. "May be best," he repeated, bringing his hand down to his face which was brown and rough-cut. His nose, chin, and cheekbones looked as though they'd been chiseled from stone by a not-too-expert sculptor.

I liked his rough-cut looks. It was one of my secret sorrows that I didn't look like him. People said I favored my mother, and if I had been a girl, that would have been fine. I would rather have been big and sort of craggy-looking like my father, instead of being small-boned with the more delicate features of my mother.

My hair is black, and soft, like my mother's, and my eyes are blue; what I really would have preferred is wiry, reddish hair like my dad's, and his amber eyes, which always looked as if there was some kind of warm fire burning back of them.

Someone knocked at the door while we were sitting in the kitchen, and when Dad said, "Come in," the door opened and attorney Frank Benz entered.

Maybe he saw how gloomy we both looked; and maybe he got a glimpse of Mother sitting in the shadows back of the potted fern; anyway, he tried to be cheerful, and said, "Now, now. The boy hasn't been convicted yet. There's plenty on our side. Just think of all the character witnesses who will swear that he's always been a good boy, one of the best. His teachers . . . The minister . . . His friends . . ." He stopped, seeing he wasn't making much of an impression.

Then he smacked his hands together as if emphasizing his words. "Anyway," he said, "just remember, it isn't the end. Capital punishment has been declared unconstitutional. The worst the boy can get will be maybe a few years in prison."

If there was a wrong thing to say, that was it. I saw my dad flinch, and the fire in his eyes begin to burn into a hot flame; and for a minute, I thought he might get up and knock Frank Benz right through a window.

Mr. Benz must have seen it, too, because he backed away and began trying to smooth it over. "What I mean is," he stuttered, "it . . . it . . . it could be a lot worse."

Gradually, the fire went out in my dad's eyes, and Mr. Benz stepped forward again. "What I came about," he said meekly, "is that we must establish exactly where Danny was at the time Jake Tabor was killed. If we can show that Danny was nowhere near the place where they found the body, they've got no case."

"You know where I was. I've told you a hundred times. I was stringing wire fence down along the marsh."

"That's right, he was," my dad said.

"Where's the marsh?" Mr. Benz asked.

"You know that, too. It's right alongside of the woods where they found Tabor's body," my dad said.

It was obvious Mr. Benz wanted to get us to change our story. When we wouldn't, his eyes wandered about the kitchen as if looking for clues—or maybe, for a way out. Then he sat down as if the air had been squeezed from him. Finally, he asked me, "Was there anyone with you?"

"Like I told you, just my dog."

"Just your dog." Mr. Benz repeated what I had said as if trying to convince himself that I really didn't have an alibi.

It was just about then that my two brothers, Jim and Jack, came bursting in through the back door. They had been at school. One is in the first grade and the other is in third, and the bus had let them out at our drive.

Ignoring both Mr. Benz and our dad, the two boys came straight to me, both asking at once, "Is it true, Danny, that you killed a guy? Is it true? Is that why you aren't in school . . . ? Because you killed a guy?"

Just for a second, I thought Dad would explode. Then Mother came hurrying from the alcove off the dining room into the kitchen; she got a hand on each boy's collar and herded them off.

"Upstairs," she said, "upstairs, and get your clothes changed."

Even when they were upstairs, we could hear their excitement. Mr. Benz was excusing himself and backing out the kitchen door, and my dad was saying to Mother, "I'll just have to have a talk with those boys. I'll just have to have a talk with them."

I went to the barn to start the chores. The cows were all up from the creek pasture, standing in the yard waiting to get into the barn to be fed and milked. They came up to the barn of their own accord in the fall, because the pasture grass was short and turning brown; and their food ration was increased since there was less to eat outside.

Jody and Tricks and Betty were in front of the door. They were as gentle as all of our soft, brown Guernseys, but they were always first . . . I took a metal bushel basket and, filling it a dozen times with silage, spread the feed along the troughs in front of the stanchions; then I opened the door and jumped back so I wouldn't get trampled as they rushed for the food.

The cows jostled each other, but they found their places, all except one of the younger ones that had only recently calved—she went right over to the pen where her calf was—and I had to take a pitchfork and gently prod her away and down the line to her place.

Once they were all in place, I closed the stanchions and lined up the milking machines. Dad came into the barn to help, and we got on with the milking.

When we finished and the milk was in the milk house cooling in the vat, we turned the cows loose again; they strung out lazily across the yard, in no big hurry to get back to the sparse pasture.

Dad and I followed them a little way so they wouldn't bunch together and mess up the yard; then, we stood for a minute at the gate and looked out across the fields down toward the woods where the body had been found. A flock of young mallards, strengthening their wings, flew across the woods and dropped from sight where the river was. We could hear geese, but we couldn't see them.

There was a touch of frost on the still air, but there were still mosquitoes, and we could hear them buzzing persistently in the still-warm, long grass beneath the fence.

I didn't feel much like talking. Maybe because it was evening. When you think of it, evening is something of a sad time. Especially an evening in autumn, not only because the day is dying, but because summer is dying, too—pretty soon all the birds will be gone, and the flowers will be dead, and most of the animals will have holed up—so there's hardly anything left except cold, and snow, and short, short days and long, long nights.

I think Dad felt it, too; but evidently, he also felt there were some things to be said.

Anyway, in an unusually quiet voice, he began. "Danny, this is a terrible, terrible thing we are faced with, and all we can do is try to meet it as best we know how, and together." He hesitated—as if he didn't know how to go on—then he started again. "As the trial starts," he said, "you're often going to feel all alone. Remember that there's your mother and me, and a lot of other good people praying for you."

He was quiet for a long time. I waited. When he talked again, it was like this: "Danny, I haven't said at all what I wanted to say. What I really want to say is this: No matter what, even if the worst comes to worst, don't give up. Remember, no matter what happens, there are good people in the world. Promise me. Promise me that no matter what happens you will always look forward to tomorrow." And then, as an afterthought, he added, "To next year. Because your life is *not* over. You've got to believe deep down inside that people are good, and that someday you will feel it, know how good they are, know how wonderful the world is . . ." He stopped talking again. He put a hand on my shoulder then, and in a whisper, said, "Just keep faith, Danny. Keep faith. Believe that there will be some brighter, better days. You must. No matter what."

10

What could I say? What could anyone say? He, too, was afraid I'd be convicted. How could I explain to him that it was not really myself I was so worried about at the moment, but them—Mother and Dad and my two brothers.

That's what I wanted to tell him. That's what I wanted him to know. But I didn't. Instead, I said: "Dad, there's something you don't know about. Something neither you nor Mr. Benz knows about. It's something you both should know. Something I should have told you right away."

Dad had been looking out toward where the sun had set, leaving long slashes of red on the horizon. He turned to me sharply and looked me straight in the eye; but then, before he could ask what I had to tell him, I went on and said: "Jake Tabor's dog, Molly, is down in the woods. She was down there the day Tabor was killed. Her pups were born down there under a brushpile. I found them. I've been feeding her. I was down there that Friday—on the day they say Jake was killed."

Neither of us said a word. His shoulders just slumped. His head hung. To the west, colors in the sky faded and the darkness moved in around us.

2 I didn't want to go back down into the woods where Tabor's body had lain, but all that night I thought about the dog down there with her pups—and, how could she find food?

Lying there in the dark, I could see a star through the window, and it moved until it was gone. Another star moved over to take its place.

I could, of course, put the pups in a basket and bring them up to the barn. Molly would probably follow along, but if anyone found out I had the dog, that would be still another strike against me. For sure, even my friends might begin to think that just possibly I really was the one who had killed Jake.

No, I couldn't bring her and the pups up to the barn, but I couldn't let her starve either.

The clock downstairs in the living room struck two, and I still wasn't asleep. I thought maybe a glass of warm milk might help, so I got up and in my bare feet padded down the steps to the kitchen.

I didn't turn on a light, but opened the refrigerator in the dark and reached for the milk. I was getting a saucepan to warm it in when I heard someone coming.

It was my mother. She had on a long, white nightgown, and her slippered feet made a whispering sound on the kitchen linoleum.

"I was just going to have a little milk," I whispered.

"Let me fix it for you," she said.

She poured a glass for herself, too, and then we sat at the table where a little starlight came through a window. I could smell the fresh, lemony odor of the lotion she used, and the heavier smell of her long, black hair.

She had the hair in braids, and the ends were tied with tiny, white ribbons. I couldn't see her face clearly enough to guess what she was thinking, but I didn't have to. I knew what she was thinking. I knew what we were all thinking.

13

We were thinking that what had happened couldn't be true. That murder could be no part of a family which went decently about its own business. That this whole thing was a strange nightmare which would pass as soon as we could bring ourselves to wake up.

But at the very moment that I told myself it was only a bad dream, I knew it was true. Because there we sat in the dark kitchen, drinking warm milk because we couldn't sleep, because we might never sleep as well as we once had. And then, when it was over . . . the thought made me shiver—when it was over . . .

Yes, when it was over? Then what?

My mother put down her glass, and I could see it was empty.

I must have slept for a few hours, but my mind wouldn't go down into the deep well of sleep. It seemed to float right up near the top, ready to surface and bring me awake.

When I did wake up, it was to look out on one of those dismal, dark days which let you know for sure winter isn't far off.

I didn't get up right away, but lay there thinking—mostly about Molly and her pups, and what was I going to do about them?

It was a cinch I couldn't admit to anyone that I knew the dog and her pups were down there.

14

It would surely look—along with everything else—
that I had been hiding them from Jake. The district attorney would be sure to say that it was just
one more reason for me to want to get rid of the
man.

But—if I didn't tell somebody or I didn't
bring them to the barn, I was going to have to feed
them—I just couldn't let them starve.

After the chores and breakfast, without my
asking, and just as if he'd been thinking about it,
too, Dad said: "For the time being, you'll just have
to feed her. Then we'll decide what to do."

He pulled on his jacket and announced:
"Well, we've got to keep going. I'll get on with the
fall plowing. When you get around to it, you can
start hauling manure out onto the stubble. We'll
plant it to corn next spring."

Spring! Next spring. When he said it, I got a
funny feeling. Here he was talking about spring
planting, just as though I were going to be with him
to help.

I shook myself like a dog trying to get water
out of his coat. I had to think about next spring
and corn-planting time. I had to think about how
I'd leave wide hedgerows for the pheasants to build
nests. I had to, I told myself, as I came out into the
kitchen on my way outside.

Standing on the steps, I could hear the tractor; so, I knew Dad was already plowing. I started

toward the barn, deciding to clean it, and to think about what I'd have to do about Molly.

As I walked, I knew there was nothing to think about. I knew that I'd already decided, and since I had, why didn't I get on with it, get it over with?

So I went to the shed where we kept scratch for the chickens, where bags of bran were stacked, and where I kept Panther's dog chow. Pulling an old gunny sack down from a two-by-four, I pounded the dust out of it, with the empty coffee can poured about four pounds of niblets into the sack, and started off across the fields.

At the edge of the woods, I sat down. I wanted to make sure no one was around and watching. I had come all the way from the barnyard along a thick hedgerow. On one side was wheat stubble and, on the other, cropped alfalfa.

Juncos were flitting through the stubble, their tiny tails flashing white, and I could see the two butter-yellow breasts of meadowlarks in the alfalfa. Otherwise, there was nothing except the sound of crows quarreling somewhere in the woods, and from far away, possibly across the river, a dog barked as if it had driven something to ground and now needed help digging it out.

Still I waited, watching the fringe of the woods for movement. The eye needs movement before it can focus clearly in a place so crowded with tree trunks.

16

There was no movement. Not even in the trees, because the leaves were down. I got up and stood for awhile. Satisfied that no one was near, I walked down and into the woods.

The woods were dreary beneath the gray sky, dreary as I'd pictured the Scottish moors from some poems and stories I'd read. Walking along among the fallen leaves, it seemed as if I was playing a part . . . being an actor in a fantastically weird story about some boy who'd murdered a man and was now sneaking back to the scene of the crime to feed the man's dog.

I wondered if I would ever be able to place myself—for very long—into the role of the accused. Or, if I would still have the weird feeling that it was happening to someone else even if I was convicted and sent to prison.

It was ridiculous, of course, but that was the way it was: unreal, dreamy, shadowy—like being waist-deep in a dense fog—never feeling the ground underfoot.

I suppose Molly smelled me long before I got a glimpse of her because she was at the brush-pile; I could tell by the expression around her eyes, and by the way she held her ears, that she'd been waiting.

She was a beautiful animal. Her long ears were black and tan, with almost golden edges. She had hound dog's eyes—deep, dark, unfathomable —in which were hidden all the mysteries of her

17

wild heritage. Even now, though she'd been in the woods and suckling five pups beneath the brushpile, her hide was a sleek black along her back, and her underparts were soft tan. Her muzzle was long. Her flews hung in a loose, kindly way to give her a benign expression.

When I called softly, she came slowly, low to the ground, as if not quite sure that she should.

"It's okay, Molly," I tried to reassure her. "It's okay."

When she was close, I put a hand to her high-domed head. It was like touching velvet. She cringed a little at my touch, and I thought of the dead Jake Tabor.

"I suppose he beat you," I said. (Tabor had a reputation for being cruel.) Molly looked up at me. "You must be hungry," I added, standing upright and walking over to the brushpile.

When I dumped the food on the ground, she only stood looking—though I knew she must be starved—so I stepped back. She came to the food slowly, deliberately.

"Eat now," I urged. She put her head down, but instead of wolfing the food, as most hungry dogs would, she took precise, tiny mouthfuls, and instead of swallowing immediately, chewed the niblets first.

While she was eating, I got to my knees and crawled into the little tunnel she had made be-

18

neath the brush. She must have left the food then, because I heard her back of me. "It's okay, Molly." I tried to let her know I wouldn't hurt the pups. But she took a leg end of my jeans between her short, front teeth and pulled. "It's okay, Molly," I repeated; but evidently she wasn't convinced, because she kept on pulling.

I let her pull, because she wasn't even tearing the material, but when I got to where she'd made a nest of leaves, I stopped, and she let me go.

I brushed away the leaves and there, in a warm bundle of black and tan, five pups were huddled. Their eyes had opened and were plum-colored. When I put a hand among them, they squirmed and whined, and one found my finger and began sucking it as though it had found one of its mother's teats.

When Molly heard her pups whine, she again closed her teeth over the end of my pants and pulled. I put leaves back over the pups and backed out.

"You've done yourself proud, Molly," I said, sitting down and looking over to where she sat watching me. "A nice bunch of pups."

With the immediate threat to her family over, Molly got up and went back to the food. I crawled a little way, so I could put my back against the trunk of a linden tree, and sat watching.

From time to time, Molly looked up from

19

the food to gaze into my eyes. I wondered what she was thinking. Or wasn't she capable of thought, as some people claimed?

Why, Molly might even know who killed Jake Tabor. She was down here the day he was killed. Maybe even lying quietly in the brush watching while the grisly act of murder was being committed.

The idea that Molly might know came to me gradually. I hadn't even considered the possibility before. In fact, we had all been so shocked and suffocated by the circumstances which had made me the number one suspect that none of us had asked the other: "Who really did kill Jake Tabor!"

Then, in that instant, the thought slammed at me like thunder. Yes, who had killed Jake Tabor? Since I hadn't, then it had to be someone else, and if we could find who that someone else was, I would be free and clear—exonerated!

Maybe that was the only way. Maybe, instead of concentrating on a way to prove that I hadn't committed the crime, we ought to be concentrating on finding the person who did.

It was a pretty good bet that Sheriff Dobbie Stotz wasn't going to explore any avenues, except those leading to my conviction. Both he and the district attorney obviously were convinced that I was their man.

Perhaps, at first, even they couldn't believe

20

that a normally quiet, usually well-behaved farm boy could kill anyone. When the evidence started coming in—the alleged threat, the knife, the footprints, my proximity to the scene of the crime—maybe then they began to look at me in a new light. Maybe that's when they became convinced I was their man.

"But it was someone else," I said quietly to the dog. "It was someone else, Molly, and maybe you know who it was."

At the sound of my voice, Molly stopped eating and looked up again. "If you could only talk. Or, if there was only some way I could get inside that mind of yours . . ." I stopped talking. But the more I thought about it, the more I became convinced that Molly might know, because, from her, no forest could keep its secrets.

Even if she hadn't seen the crime committed, no one could possibly enter or leave the woods without her nose telling her about it. Her nose was even more reliable than her eyes. Her nose could catalog every person she had ever met in a special section of her brain. And along with that positive identification, there would be stored other valuable nuggets of information as: Was the man friend or foe? Was he cruel or kind . . . ?

"Molly! Molly!" I said, helplessly. "You know . . . I'm sure you know. I'm positive that you at least smelled whoever it was that came into the woods that day to kill Jake Tabor. I know you did. But you can't tell me, can you? You can't tell me. You can't tell me. Oh, Molly, if you only could!" I caught myself. I had been babbling.

The chain of events leading up to my arrest for Jake Tabor's killing began the first week in September at the Tri-state Coon Dog Trial.

3

Molly shouldn't have been running that day. She was at least eight weeks pregnant and bulging with pups. Only Jake Tabor could have done a thing like that.

"Best line and tree dog in the country," he had boasted, "so now she's going to earn her keep!" The stakes were high—five hundred dollars, not counting side bets—and everybody said Jake had put down a bundle.

When he brought the dog to the line, there was a murmur of dissent from the gallery. When Jake saw the faces of the judges, he said, "Look, I've figured it close. Those pups aren't due for a week yet."

Well, maybe Jake had figured it right, and maybe he hadn't. But to run a dog already that burdened was nothing short of a crime. Ted Feldman, one of the judges, held up the start of the stake, saying, "Sure you want to run her, Jake? Looks to me she's due to whelp any minute."

"You going to disqualify her?" Jake shot back.

"No," Feldman said, "there's no rule I know of whereby we can disqualify her. It's just that she might get hurt and hurt the pups in the bargain."

Tabor, a red-eyed little man with a scraggly beard, thrust his face forward and said, "Well, you stick to your judging, Feldman, and I'll worry about my dog."

Molly had turned her back on the line and was looking at the gallery because of the sound of angry voices coming from it. Jake jerked her around, half lifting her off the ground, and said, "Let's get started!"

There were twenty-two dogs from three states in the stake. Blueticks, redbones, foxhounds, black-and-tan, greyhound and bloodhound crosses . . . some real mixtures.

24

Molly was a black-and-tan, a small dog by most hound dog standards, and she looked smaller than she actually was because she had a way of stalking low, like a cat ready to spring. The thing which distinguished her was the fire in her eyes, a fire lighted by the live coals of desire to stay out ahead of the pack, to come first to the treed coon so she could put her paws on the trunk and bell out her victory.

Feldman had gone back after the rebuff to consult the other two judges. People in the gallery couldn't hear what they were saying, but they must have agreed that there was no way they could disqualify Molly; if Jake wanted to kill his dog, that was his business.

Of course, I wasn't there when all this happened. But I heard it so many times that I imagined I could see the uplifted eyebrows of some women who had been standing by.

The afternoon they ran the dogs, I was bringing in a third cutting of alfalfa because fall was in the air, the hay was down, school would be starting soon, and then, my dad would get little help out of me except for the chores.

I heard the dogs start, and although I'm mainly a duck hunter and a Labrador man, that was some pretty savage singing, and I could feel the hairs on my arms lift. I noticed I was suddenly breathing hard with excitement. Of all the wild

25

wonders, there's maybe nothing that tugs at a guy's guts like the sound of a hound bugling full down a hot trail. Panther was with me, and when he heard the hounds, even though he's a black Lab who has been trained to retrieve ducks he started off as if to join them—I had to call him back.

I saw the hounds later, strung out across the marshy bottoms where our land comes down to the river, but they were too far away for me to know if Molly was still running, or if she'd already broken off and disappeared. From my lookout atop the load of loose hay, I could see all the way down the slope, and it was like looking through the wrong end of a pair of binoculars—they were that far away.

Still, I could distinguish the two deer that came bounding out of the thick woods which border on the water, and I saw two dogs shunt off to chase the whitetails.

And that's what they said when Molly wasn't at the coon tree. They said she'd broken off—taken a deer track to run right out of the country.

They told me it made Jake Tabor roaring mad. "Molly's deer-proof!" he insisted. "She's deer-proof, rabbit-proof, and she won't even take off on a 'possum. Nothing, I tell you. Nothing but coons."

"Well, where is she then?" the other hound dog men asked.

26

"Somebody picked her up. That's what. Someone stole her," Jake said.

I don't know if they laughed at him. I don't think people who knew Jake Tabor would, not to his face, anyway. Why ask for trouble?

Provoking Jake was as senseless as teasing one of the timber rattlers which we sometimes find among the river bluffs. It's best to walk around them—unless you're going to kill them—and, of course, nobody I knew hated Jake quite enough to kill him.

That's what I thought, anyway. So it was a surprise when they found him dead . . . stab wounds in the neck . . . lying on his back in a cedar grove in what everyone calls Black Haw Woods.

It happened a couple days after he came to our farm hunting for the dog. He had his boy, Matt, and Bob Bacon, a drifter from Coulee City with him.

Matt, in some ways, reminded me of Molly. I suppose that isn't really a good comparison, but Jake completely dominated the boy as he did his hounds, and I wouldn't doubt that he whipped Matt whenever it suited his purpose. That's what I thought I saw in Matt's eyes, a sort of fear that, at any moment, his father might lash out without warning either with a word or a whip. Of course, I could have been wrong.

Bacon seemed like a kind of zero. Not that it was his fault. Maybe he just despised himself, because he knew anybody could buy him or his services for just one bottle of booze.

I'm not about to set myself up as a judge of men, but it seems to me that Jake Tabor had Bob Bacon right in his back pocket; and maybe it made him feel good to keep him there.

Anyway, after I told them Molly was not in the barn or in any of the other buildings, Jake went on looking anyway. Then, when Matt and Bob held back, standing in the doorway, he went over, got Matt by the scruff of the neck, and pushed him toward the stairs, saying, "Now, get you. Get up in that haymow and look around." When Bacon didn't move, Tabor lifted an arm toward him and said, "You, too!"

I suppose that was the moment at which I should have told Jake that Molly was down in the woods, that her pups were under the brushpile. I don't know why I held back, unless it was because I couldn't bring myself to turn the dog over to a man who would run her when she was so burdened with pups.

Even so, probably nothing would have come of the incident if Jake hadn't started lighting matches. When he couldn't see in the silo, he lighted a match. I protested right away. "You'll burn the barn down," I said. "It's full of hay. It'll go up like a bomb."

"Then drag that dog out and we'll be on our way," he said.

28

I told him he was crazy, that I didn't have his dog. If I sounded brave, I wasn't. Confronting Jake was like confronting one of those rattlers. You knew that if you got too close, the snake would strike.

Jake had slid back the door to an attached granary, and was lighting matches to look in when Matt and Bob came thumping down the stairs from the loft.

"Too dark to see much up there," Bacon said.

Jake slammed the door to the grain room and came over. "Well, we'll go back and take a closer look," he said.

That's when I jumped in the way. "You're crazy. . . . You'll stir up enough dust to cause an explosion!"

Jake gave me a shove and said, "Out of my way, kid."

I jumped back in front of him, and he grabbed me by the shoulders.

"You wanna get hurt?" he threatened.

"You can't light matches up there," I shouted, and shoved at Jake's body. He grabbed me, rammed me back, and banged my head against a stanchion.

That might have ended it, except Panther came through the door and, when he saw Jake handling me, he growled.

I doubt that Panther would have bitten

him, but Jake thought he was going to, because he gave the dog such a hard kick in the head he sent him reeling across the barn floor.

That did it. I jumped Tabor, but I was no match for him; he slammed me back against the stanchion again. This time, the metal top bar cut my head and blood squirted. When Jake saw the blood, he turned and said, "Let's get out of here."

I sat down, dizzy and weak, but when the three of them went through the door, I yelled: "Jake Tabor, someday somebody is going to kill you. You hear me, Jake? Someday somebody is going to kill you!"

That's all I said, and that's exactly the way I said it, but when they came to arrest me for Jake's murder, Bacon and Matt Tabor put it another way. They told the sheriff I said: "Jake Tabor, someday *I'm* going to kill you. You hear me, Jake? Someday *I'm* going to kill you!"

Then, on top of it, they found my jackknife not far from where they found the body. I'll admit there probably was blood on it, but it wasn't Jake Tabor's blood.

And so it was with the footprints. Sure, they were mine. I had been all over that part of the woods. When they measured my bird shooters against the bootprints, they fit the mold exactly. Why not? They were mine. I'd been down there. Often. Right now, if you look, you'll still find my

prints on the soft ground—in the marsh mud—
along the shore where Bloodstone River runs.

I told them how the knife got down there,
but the district attorney only laughed. He emphasized, "But it's human blood on that knife, the
same type of blood which once ran in Jake Tabor's
veins."

It all mystified me, since I knew it wasn't
human blood. I told them that, but they wouldn't
believe me. Nor would they believe it when I said
that Matt Tabor and Bob Bacon were liars, that I
had *not* threatened Jake Tabor, that I hadn't said
". . . someday *I'm* going to kill you . . . ," but
rather, ". . . someday *somebody* is going to kill
you. . . ."

So there's my name in the paper. There's my
picture on the front page of the *Coulee City Cour-
ier*. And there's my mother sitting in the shadows
with tears on her cheeks; and there's my father
going around with a hard ridge of muscle showing
on each cheek, and his mouth in such a hard
straight line you can't even see his lips.

So there it is: the crowd silent on the courthouse steps as I come out the door after the preliminary hearing—after the decision to try me as an
adult instead of a juvenile. There it is: with people
looking at me out of the sides of their eyes, never
turning full face, always seeming to sidle away from
me.

There it is: school goes on without me, and scarcely anyone comes to visit the farm anymore. There it is: the telephone rarely rings; and nights, I awaken sweating; and I push away my mother's cake; and the shades are drawn; and Panther looks up at me with bewilderment.

There it is. All around me. The specter, the feeling of guilt. But God help me, because I didn't do it. I didn't kill Jake Tabor.

As usual, I couldn't sleep that night, except that now there was a difference. Instead of self-pity and bewilderment, my mind kept coming **4** back to the thought that Molly surely knew who killed Jake Tabor.

I doubted that anyone could enter Black Haw Woods without Molly knowing it. So, back of those dark eyes was locked away the secret to my salvation—written there in the gray wrinkles of Molly's brain was a distinct and individual impression of how the man smelled, and she would never forget it. Dogs never do.

But there was no way to go about unlocking such a misty, mysterious thing as a hound dog's mind. It was like looking at a star which is many million miles away, hoping, that in a twinkle of its shining light, it will suddenly reveal all the secrets of the universe. It just couldn't happen, although it took me until four o'clock in the morning to convince myself that there was no way, no way at all, of getting beneath the black velvet of that beautiful head.

I felt relaxed after I'd made up my mind that there was no way of enlisting Molly's help in solving the crime—not good, but relaxed. I didn't have to struggle anymore with myself, and could lie back convinced that there wasn't much to do except wait, and maybe pray.

I was just falling asleep, drifting down from the high excitement of my mental explorations to the quiet valley of resignation when a noise at the window brought me back wide awake. I sat up in bed and looked at the window and listened to what sounded like the tracings of many small fingers down the length of the pane. When the soft sound continued, I threw back the blankets and got up. Then, even before I got to the window, I knew. It was snow, the first snow of the season, coming in on the wind.

I knelt down in front of the window and rested my chin on the sill. Outside, the one night light up over the barn was almost lost in a white swirl of flakes. Beneath—in the mud—the prints of boots, cattle's hooves, and Panther's paws, and the tracings of chickens' feet were being painted over. Even while I watched, they all disappeared, and the dark earth became like white fleece just shorn from one of our sheep.

The steady procession of flakes had a hypnotic effect on me, and I felt my eyes closing. I dreamed that I was down in the woods sitting by the brushpile carrying on a conversation with Molly. She was talking as coherently as any human, except when she'd begin to tell me who had murdered Jake—her voice would fade, and I could never get the name.

When I awakened, I was cold and stiff. The snow had stopped falling, and a gray day was dawning. I was rigid with cold and got up carefully, bracing myself from chair to bedpost and then crawling beneath the covers to shiver myself warm.

No one was in the kitchen when I came downstairs so I pulled on my boots and a heavy jacket and went outside. My dad's tracks, with Panther's paw prints alongside, went from the steps across the yard and disappeared into the barn. I could hear the milking machine, so I knew he was already doing chores. I hurried to help.

Just inside the barn door, I stood for a moment, letting the odor of warm cattle and the rich scent of hay wash over me and comfort me the way barn smells always had a way of doing. I can't say why I felt I could always shed my problems in the barn. Maybe it was the feeling of permanency, the feeling that here things didn't change much, and that, when we were all gone, there would still be cows to milk and cats running alongside begging for milk—on and on, maybe forever.

While I stood there, Panther came up to say good morning, and then my father came with the first pail of frothy milk. I said good morning to both and pitched in to help with the chores.

After breakfast, I waited for Dad to announce our work plan for the day, but when he asked if I wanted to go to Coulee City with my mother I said, "No. Maybe I'll just visit Molly and check the creek and the river for mink and muskrat signs to get some idea where to set my traps."

I took Panther with me, and I carried food for Molly. Along the hedgerow, on the way down to the woods, Panther checked out the rabbit and squirrel tracks, stopped to look back at me when he came to the paw prints of a fox, and barked a few times at a flock of snow buntings which rose and fell like white flakes, always just out of his reach.

When we entered the woods, Panther left off playing and walked purposefully toward the brushpile. He obviously had winded Molly and the pups, and I was sure that, by this time, Molly also knew that we were coming.

36

Everywhere in the woods the blanket of snow lay like the white pages of a book where the night animals had left their signatures. There were also scribblings by some blue jays, and funny, pigeon-toed footnotes left by a couple crows . . . and then—like a stranger who has come suddenly uninvited into the house—there were the tracks of a man.

I stopped as though I'd been hit. Man tracks! Fresh tracks—made sometime after dawn. Circling, it seemed, as if searching. I stood examining them. Worn soles—only the faint trace of a boot tread.

Panther followed the tracks a little way and then came back. Whose? Whose tracks were they? What was he doing down here?

Well, first there was Molly. Having smelled us, she would be waiting. Panther was already proceeding in the direction of the brushpile, so I followed.

When I got to the brushpile, Molly wasn't waiting for me. I knelt in front of the tunnel she had made and saw her cringing far back as though expecting to be punished.

Whoever had been roaming the woods had frightened her, that much was apparent. Panther put his head into the tunnel and wagged his tail. Molly growled. Panther whined, almost apologetically, and then backed away as though to invite her out.

37

Still she cringed in the lair she had fashioned, but the pups, on scenting Panther, came tumbling out.

Molly came out then and, snarling and punishing with her teeth, tried to drive them back. When they wouldn't go, I walked back a ways and called Panther to my side. Then the pups followed Molly back beneath the brushpile; after dumping out the dog food, I went back to where the man tracks were.

The tracks led toward the river. They meandered, as though whoever had made them was searching for something. Near the river, they doubled back, coming almost all the way to the brushpile where Molly had hidden the pups.

By now, I knew the tracks were not those of a neighboring farmer. It was obvious the tracks had been made by a man more accustomed to walking on concrete than along the uneven terrain of a woodland.

The man had stumbled often. He had blundered into stands of prickly ash and, at one point, had been forced to back out and seek a different route.

The trail led right to the place where the sheriff claimed Tabor's body had been lying, although now there was nothing to indicate that a murder had been committed here.

At this point, however, the meandering trail

straightened out and went directly to the line fence. The man had ducked beneath the wire, so I assumed he was not too tall.

Well, at least I knew two things about him. He probably was short, and he likely lived in town.

I went under the fence and continued trailing. Panther seemed to have gotten the idea, and now he went from bootprint to bootprint snuffing loudly to clear the snow from his nostrils so he could get a sharp impression of the man's smell.

At the railroad tracks the trail turned south toward Coulee City. I could see that the man had slipped often, and once he had fallen, leaving the imprint of his body in the snow.

My guess about his size had been right. He was short. What's more, he had not been wearing gloves because there was a clear imprint where he'd put a hand down to lift himself.

Now, I asked myself, who would run around in cold, snowy woods without gloves? Surely, no farmer; and surely, no hunter, at least, not a hunter of any experience.

The rooftops of Coulee City were coming into view when I spotted the man far down the tracks. If I wanted to get a look at him before he disappeared into the maze of city streets, I would have to hurry.

I broke into a trot. Panther was delighted and ran back and forth in front of me, yipping as if

39

we were playing some kind of game. The man must have heard the dog and looked back, because he began running.

I'd never catch him now. He would disappear in the city long before I could get near enough to see who he was. I slowed to a walk and then stopped. Within seconds, the figure turned in at the lumber yard and was gone. I took off my cap and wiped the sweat from my forehead. As I turned to retrace my steps, my eyes caught the bright shine of an object in the snow. I went down from the roadbed into the ditch.

It was a wine bottle, a pint bottle from the Coulee City Central Liquor Store. The word "Muscatel" was printed in large black letters on the label.

Whoever had been prowling through my woods liked wine. Coulee City had a lot of winos, more than its share since the hard maple had all been cut and the bowling pin factory had closed. Any one of them might have taken the notion to go wandering about the countryside. Their antics sometimes defied explanation. The *Coulee City Chronicle* rarely printed a paper but that one or another of these unfortunate derelicts wasn't the object of some sort of police action.

Panther seemed disappointed when we didn't continue on down the trail. It was a sort of game for him, like looking for a cow which had wandered off into the brakes to have her calf and then hiding it so we'd have to track her down to bring them both back.

The snow had begun to melt when I went back across the open fields which bordered the tracks. By the time I got to the woods, the clouds had drifted away and the sun was shining.

Molly had eaten most of the food, so when Panther went over to help himself to what remained, I didn't stop him.

"Who was in the woods?" I asked Molly, as she sat there watching Panther eat. "Anyone you know?"

The little hound turned her head from side to side as she caught the question in my tone of voice.

"If you could talk," I continued, "I'm sure we could solve everything and save my skin in the bargain."

The sun was hot enough so I had to take off my jacket. I laid it across a log and sat beside it. Panther, having finished the food, came over and nudged my hand, a gesture he used when he wanted his ears scratched.

"Go scratch your own ears," I told him. "I've got things to think about."

But, of course, there wasn't much profit in thinking, because how could it help? Some short, city-bred, wine-drinking fellow had been walking in my woods, and it could have been one of maybe twenty or even thirty men who lived along Water Street.

I whistled softly to Molly, and she came crawling over on her belly. I put out a hand, and she licked it with her warm tongue.

"Nice Molly," I encouraged her. "Good dog."

She lifted to her feet and put her chin on my jacket pocket, the one in which the wine bottle was. At once, her ears went back, her tail came tight to her flanks, and she slunk away.

"You don't like that smell?" I asked, bringing the bottle out of the pocket.

The dog stood at the entrance to her den. I got up and walked over holding the bottle out in front of me. She turned and crawled quickly beneath the brushpile.

"So what does that mean?" I formulated the words in my mind. Probably nothing, because surely the dog would have come to fear the smell of wine. Likely Jake was always a little drunk when he whipped her. She probably had come to associate the odor of alcohol with the threat of punishment.

Maybe it wasn't even that meaningful. Some dogs just hate the odor of alcohol. I had seen it before—seen dogs shy away from a trainer or handler who'd been drinking.

Good handlers never drank, not while they were running their dogs.

42

NO MAN FOR MURDER

I put the wine bottle back in the jacket pocket, whistled to Panther, and started east along the hedgerow toward home.

5 It was that night that I first heard
Molly. I was snuggled down in the
feather tick my grandmother had
made many years ago, thinking about
how life can suddenly turn from its well-worn path
down a rugged trail of misadventure and nightmares.

When I first heard the dog, I didn't recognize the sound, it was so far off. As it came to me,
up out of the woods and across the long fields, it
sounded like the wail of a banshee right out of a
horror story—thin and painful, ". . . rising and
falling like the mournful lament of an eternally

searching soul." The last I had read in some book or other; it had stayed with me and pretty well described the sound.

I shivered then, even though the warm, feathery quilt was enveloping me almost like a cocoon does a caterpillar . . . I said to myself: "What kind of creature is that?"

Then Molly must have come up out of a valley to run along a ridge, because the eerie, quavering howl changed to a bell-like bugling, and I knew she was hunting.

It made sense. The pups were four or five weeks old, ready to abandon her breast for more solid food.

So, what would a healthy, well-fed coon dog be doing if not hunting raccoons? Back of her were generations of hunting dogs, bred only to trail and then triumphantly announce in bold, clear tones that they were doing their duty, and this is where the hunted was running—over this hill, along this ridge, through this swamp, over this creek . . .

The spooky feeling had vanished. I even felt myself thrill to the sound of the chase. In my mind's eye, I could even see the coon, ambling along like a little bear, looking back from time to time, perhaps snarling.

I could see Molly with ears flapping, tail wagging wildly, legs thrusting her along the scent line—through the bushes, across the clearings, among the trees—head down to gulp in the hot, strong scent—muzzle lifting about every dozen steps to bay about how it was.

I was wide awake by now, and then a shadow in my doorway turned out to be Dad, and he asked, "Is that Molly?"

"It's her all right," I said.

"Too bad, because now someone is sure to find her."

"Someone will sooner or later, anyway," I said, and then added, "There were man tracks down there today. Could be somebody is looking for her."

"Well, maybe it would be best if she were found. As long as she's down there, and so long as you're feeding her, she's a threat. People will think *you've* been hiding her."

"I suppose so," I said.

He turned to go back to his bedroom, but not without first telling me to try to get some sleep.

The next day I didn't get down to the woods to feed Molly. Instead, I went to town because I needed a new suit for the trial. Buying a new suit for a murder trial seemed ridiculous to me, but Frank Benz insisted on it.

"He's got to look his best. We don't have much of a case, but at least we can show him off to the jury as the kind of boy who couldn't possibly commit such a heinous crime."

I didn't know what "heinous" meant, but it did seem to me that a new suit was a little like lying, sort of putting on a false front, when all we wanted was to tell the plain, simple truth and hope the jury would believe me, and believe that Bob Bacon and Matt Tabor were lying when they said I had threatened to kill Jake.

I knew the clothing salesman, and he was too polite. His whole attitude was one of forbearance. It was just as if he knew that I was guilty but that he was going to give me the benefit of the doubt—at least until the jury came in with a verdict.

I felt pretty low by the time the suit had been selected—a navy blue—and I walked out of the store with the suit box under my arm.

It was the same thing at the "Krafty Kitchen" where we had lunch. Sally Moraine, the waitress, was overly solicitous. Instead of just bringing our hamburgers and French fries, she kept filling our water glasses, asking if we wanted anything else, and looking at me with bright eyes as if to say, "We're all behind you, Danny, even if you did do it, because Jake was no good, and maybe he deserved dying."

I was glad to get back to the farm. But even in my room, I couldn't shed the icy feeling which comes, I suppose, from having been set aside by the town's people—temporarily "put on ice"—to be kept there until the verdict was in and they could feel and express their sorrow because I was going to jail, or rejoice with me because I'd been set free.

It grew dark while I sat in my room, and I could hear the milk machine out in the barn; I knew I should go out and help Dad. Still, I sat, and as Dad had predicted, I suddenly felt all alone and lonely, as if the whole world was convinced I was the killer and had turned its back on me.

I might have sat there the whole evening letting the sadness seep down into my bones, but my mother appeared in the doorway. She didn't turn on a light, but she said, "Perhaps, you ought to go out and help your father. I've got supper ready and, if he has to do the chores alone, it will get cold."

So I got up and went out into the barn, and as always, the close, crowding warmth of animals surrounded by their own body fragrance gave me that special feeling of peace and calm. So by the time the chores were done, the edge of sadness had been softened, and when the cows had been turned out of the barn and I had switched the light off, my appetite was back and I felt that I could go on living again.

Molly ran again that night, but how can I explain how she sounded and how I felt? Mostly, I suppose I had the feeling that I would like to be out there running with her. It seemed that if I could hide as she was hiding in a brushpile in the woods, the entire terrible affair of Jake Tabor would just fade away.

Being a dog had its drawbacks, but it also had its advantages. For one thing, Molly wasn't worrying, and that was because she wasn't living for tomorrow but for the excitement of the moment. If she had to hide all day, she was free to roam at night; and then, if any sadness might linger, she quickly rid herself of it, and bugling at the top of her voice, did the thing she loved most and could do so magnificently—trail a coon over, under, through, and around any and all obstacles.

I drifted off to sleep after awhile, and the last thing I heard before I fell asleep was her clear bell tones coming so far across the country I knew she must be down in the mud of the marsh along the river—probably putting migrating ducks up from their night camps and shivering a whole valley of wildlings with her headlong hunt.

Frank Benz came over the next day. The trial had been scheduled. Dad got up and looked at the calendar. "December second," he said, "that's a Monday."

"Well, I'll be glad to get it over with," I said.

Frank Benz had been looking down at his hands, but after awhile he looked across the table at my father and me. "The district attorney has made me a proposition," he finally said.

49

He waited. My father prompted him, "Yes?"

The attorney cleared his throat, then said, "He'll accept a plea of second degree murder—murder brought on by serious provocation."

I wouldn't have let him go on that long, except that, at first, I was stunned. When I found my voice, I shouted, "Plead guilty! Is everybody crazy? Plead guilty when I didn't do it!"

My father was up and had an arm around my shoulder. I could feel the hot blood in my face. I looked up into his eyes. He looked into mine. Then he turned toward the attorney and said, "He'll never plead guilty. Not ever. Not to any charge of killing anyone." He said it flatly, without emotion.

"Then what?" the attorney threw up his hands. "We've got nothing—not even an alibi. They've got everything. The boy threatened the man. He was in the area at the time the murder was committed. They found his bootprints right there. They even found a knife—and he says it is his—and there was blood on it!"

I shouted then, "Yes, they found blood on it. But it wasn't Jake's blood. It was rabbit blood."

Frank Benz shook his head sadly. "They tested it. It was Jake's blood."

How could it be? Jake's blood on my knife? It couldn't be! That wasn't Jake's blood. It was the blood of a rabbit Panther had run into a rockpile. It was blood of a rabbit I had caught and gutted to take home to make rabbit stew. It was not Jake's blood.

I told the attorney so, but he just shook his head. "It was not rabbit's blood. It was Jake's blood. I saw the laboratory report."

Jake's blood on my knife! It couldn't be. After gutting the rabbit, I must have laid the knife down on a rock while I wiped out the cavity of the rabbit with grass. That's when I must have forgotten to pick it up.

So how could it be Jake's blood? How could it be?

I looked at my dad. He reached out and put a hand on my forearm. Then he looked at the attorney and said, "The boy will not plead guilty."

"Then what?" the attorney said, throwing both hands into the air as though to shed himself of the whole thing. "Everything is against him. We've got no defense. Isn't it better to go to prison for a little while than to have to go for a lifetime?"

I looked into my dad's face again. It was set hard as a rock. Nothing moved, nothing, except the thin line of his lips when he said, "He'll never plead guilty. . . . NEVER."

Now I was really desperate! At first, there had been bewilderment; then, there had been sad-

51

ness and, of course, fear. Then I had felt that I might solve the murder if I could probe Molly's mind. Then had come rejection. Still, all along, I had felt that eventually they would discover that the blood on the knife was that of a rabbit, not Jake's blood. Now, desperation.

I had to get out of the house to think. The air was crisp, cold, but it didn't clear my head. I had to walk—see Molly. I got a sack of food, whistled up Panther, and started down the hedgerow.

The pups were out when I got there. They attacked Panther with abandon, chewing his ears, nipping at his paws and tail. At first, my black dog looked bewildered. Then he entered into the spirit of the mock battle and, carefully, closed his strong jaws down on a head, a foot, or a whole black-and-tan body.

I emptied the food out of the sack, and Molly smelled it and came over. The pups must have smelled it, too, because they quit pestering Panther and crowded around Molly.

I figured it was time for them to learn to eat, so I took them one at a time—crumbling the food, forcing the crumbs into their mouths. They caught on almost at once and began to eat, if not eagerly, at least with enough enthusiasm to get a little solid nourishment.

Molly's milk supply would be drying up now, and if the pups were going to have good, strong bones, well-formed bodies, and strong sinews, they would need food, lots of it.

There was still food left when Molly suddenly stopped eating. Her head came up, and she swung it from left to right snuffing the air loudly. I looked at Panther. He had smelled something, too.

"What is it?" I whispered, just as though the dogs might somehow understand me. As if in answer, Molly tucked her tail between her legs, put her ears back, and the hair along her back bristled.

Whatever she smelled frightened her. Panther, however, exhibited only what I felt was curiosity. He ran a little upwind, snuffing loudly, and then returned.

Molly whined. It was a low and, what I thought, an anxious command. Evidently, the pups understood it since they crowded around her. When she went beneath the brushpile, they followed.

I turned to Panther. "What is it, boy?" I asked. "What is it?" I repeated in a whisper.

He caught the excitement in my voice and ran off a little way into the woods. I followed. Then when he came back to me, I took off my belt and made a short leash of it, so he couldn't go forward.

Together we proceeded carefully and quietly, stopping often to listen. Then I got a clue. Crows sounded an alarm. Coming sharp on the crisp air was the high-pitched signal. It could be a cat, fox, or an owl which was disturbing the crows, but I didn't think it likely. Such enemies usually triggered nothing but contempt from the crows, and usually, they all ganged up to dive-bomb the object of their consternation.

No, these signals were sharper, more imperative. They seemed to say: "Move out. Move out."

I found a log and sat on it to wait. The crows stopped cawing. Panther dropped down beside me, but instead of resting his muzzle on his forepaws, he kept his head high, his ears and eyes alert.

Then the woods became still, too still. I should have heard chickadees, nuthatches, woodpeckers . . . but there was nothing. I opened my mouth and cupped my hands back of my ears to amplify sound. There was nothing. An acorn dropped back of me with the shattering report of a rifle being fired. I let out my breath with a grunt, never realizing I had been holding it. Panther looked up at me. I put a hand to his head to keep him quiet.

There! Wasn't that brush being broken? I held my breath again. But there was nothing, and perhaps I had imagined it. I let my breath out slowly, softly.

Suddenly then blue jays began screaming, "Thief!" There must have been a half dozen—not more than two hundred yards from me. The clamor resounded throughout the woods. I stood up, hoping to be able to see across the top of the underbrush, but the tree trunks were too closely grouped.

The jays broke off then, stopped screaming. Once more the woods were quiet. A movement overhead caught my eye. I searched the bare branches to identify it. There was a flick of gray. Then I saw the squirrel. It had come around to my side of the tree and was flattened motionless to the trunk. If my eyes hadn't seen the flick of its tail, they would have passed over it as only a knot or the stump end of a broken branch.

Of course the squirrel was hiding, but not from me. Someone was coming straight toward me. The squirrel had come around to my side of the tree.

I got up carefully, stepped around the log, and slid down behind it. I pulled Panther with me, and then I lay waiting with only the top of my head and my eyes showing above the rough bark.

I heard leaves being scuffed about; then, I heard brush being broken. Whoever was coming was certainly not trying to conceal his presence.

I put an arm around Panther to make sure he would not get up and go forward to greet the man; then, I raised my head a little to get a better look.

It was Bob Bacon. His thin, scraggly hair

was down over his forehead nearly screening his eyes, and even from a distance, I could see the red welts left by brambles and prickly ash on his face and the backs of his hands.

His clothes were ragged and torn, and he walked with a limp—a man as alien to the forest as I suppose I was to city streets.

Although it was chilly, he sat on a stump and, with a blue handkerchief, wiped sweat from his face. Then he pulled a pint bottle, like the one I'd found alongside the tracks, from his pocket and, tilting it, took a long drink.

It was obvious he was looking for something. But what? Surely, it must be Molly.

After the bottle was back in his pocket, he got up, and when he passed, he was so close I could see the red veins in his eyes. He never saw me!

Once, I thought Panther surely would give us away. I could feel him rise, and I had to force him back down. I whispered, "Stay. Stay."

When I could no longer hear Bacon I got up. I wanted to follow him, but I was afraid the dog would betray my presence. So I headed back toward the brushpile and Molly.

That night, I talked it over with my dad. It seemed to me that it was our place to take the initiative, to try to find out who killed Jake Tabor, and probably, a good place to start with was Bob Bacon.

"He might have done it," I said to Dad, as we sat at the kitchen table sipping coffee.

"I don't think so. I don't think he'd have the courage to kill a man."

"He'd have reason enough," I said. "Jake was always making it rough for him. He was Jake's slave. He'd do anything for a bottle of wine."

"Anything but kill," Dad said. "I don't believe he would kill."

"Not even if he was drunk?"

"Then he'd never be able to. Jake would tear him to pieces."

"But what if he crept up from behind?"

"While he was drunk? Not likely. And anyway, drunk or sober, he'd not have the guts—not to kill."

"But then, what's he doing in the woods?"

My dad shrugged. "Looking for the dog, I suppose. That dog is worth money. Lots of money."

6 It is difficult to believe that the mind can go right on even while we sleep, that the subconscious mind never stops working, and sometimes, on awakening, a particularly difficult problem has been solved. I once had my doubts about that, but no more.

After Dad and I finished our coffee, we went to bed. I thrashed about for several hours, trying to understand how my knife could have Jake Tabor's blood on it. There must be a mistake, I thought. All I had done with the knife was skin out a rabbit, cut off its head and feet, and then put the knife down while I cleaned the blood off the rabbit with dry grass. So, how human blood?

The puzzling problem went around in my mind. When I fell asleep, I was still trying to understand how such an incredible thing might have happened.

I don't know how long I'd been asleep, but when I awakened, I was sitting straight up in bed and as wide awake as if I'd never slept.

"Maybe," my mind was saying, "maybe the knife with Tabor's blood on it wasn't your knife after all. Maybe . . ." I almost gasped out loud at the thought. Maybe there were two knives. Maybe there was another knife just like the one I'd lost. Maybe my knife was still down there where I'd left it!

The more I thought about it, the more sense it made. How many people had knives like the so-called murder knife? Maybe every third farmer had that very same knife. It was a common, two-bladed kind, available in almost any hardware store. So maybe mine was lying there where I'd left it on a rock next to the stone fence.

Naturally, when asked to identify the murder weapon, I had said it was mine. It looked like mine. It had been found in the woods where I'd lost mine, so why shouldn't I conclude that it was mine?

But, maybe it wasn't!

I couldn't go back to sleep. Down across the fields in the woods, I could hear Molly baying. I got up and went to the window. One of our cats, the tiger stripe, was walking stealthily through the circle of yellow from the night light. She was coming from the feed storage shed, and she had a mouse between her jaws.

Downstairs the clock struck. I counted. Three o'clock. It was still nearly three hours before dawn. I couldn't wait. I had to know. Now!

Slipping out of my pajama bottoms, I put on my clothes. My mother appeared in the doorway. "Danny, why aren't you in bed?" she asked.

"Mother, don't worry, but I have to check something out." I didn't want to go into a lengthy explanation.

She went away, and then, in a few seconds, my dad was there. "Danny, where are you going?"

"I've got an idea—about the knife. I don't think the one the sheriff's got is mine. I think my knife is still down there."

"But can't it wait until morning?" he asked.

"No, it can't. I can't sleep. I've got to check it out."

In the next room, my two brothers must have heard our voices; now I could hear Mother telling them to go back to sleep, that everything was all right.

"Well, okay, Danny . . . If you have to go . . ."

"I have to. That knife. It's the one thing we've never been able to understand—how my knife had Tabor's blood on it."

I picked up a flashlight from the window sill in the kitchen and pulled on my jacket. Panther jumped when I opened the door. He'd been sleeping in the entryway next to the warm door. When he started to follow me, I turned toward the barn. "Not tonight," I said, opening the barn door and locking him in.

I heard him whine as I crossed the yard, went through the vegetable garden gate, and then crawled between the wires of the fence to come out into the field alongside the hedgerow.

There was a moon—a curling sliver of white silver—but it shed little light. I stood still to let my eyes become accustomed to the dark. Molly was still running. A horned owl, perhaps disturbed by her persistence, hooted loudly, almost as if in anger.

Gradually, as I stood, the outlines of the hedgerow came into focus. I put the flashlight into my jacket pocket. I wouldn't need it, not walking over the relatively smooth ground of the stubble field.

Halfway along, and just at the crest of a rise which let me look down on the indistinct mass that marked the woods, a rush of sound stopped me in my tracks. I could feel my heart jump with excitement, and it was a few seconds before my mind told it to beat quietly, that the flurry was only of wings, wings of birds, disturbed on their roosts in the wild plum trees in the hedgerow.

By the time I got to the woods, the moon had dropped back of the trees and taken what little light there had been with it. Even so, I could make out the dim path I had worn through the brush on my visits to Molly.

I went slowly, carefully, with an arm crooked in front of my face to keep from being slapped by branches. When I got to the brushpile, all the pups came tumbling out to greet me. I brought out the flashlight and turned it on them. They whined excitedly, if from hunger, or fright, or perhaps, loneliness, I couldn't tell.

I took the time to kneel and pet each one, and then I headed north toward the stone fence where I'd gutted the rabbit. When the pups started to follow, I tried to shoo them back beneath the brush. When they wouldn't go, I rushed at them, and in a reproving voice, scolded. They tumbled over one another yelping, and then all disappeared beneath the brushpile.

I went the rest of the way to the fence without a light; then, I turned it on to examine the stones. I wasn't sure. In the dark, things looked different. Leaving the light on, I followed the path of white—examining the barrier as I walked—hoping I would recognize the place where I'd lifted the stones to get my hands on the rabbit.

I walked all the way to the east end where barbed wire took over, and then retracing my steps, walked all the way to the west end without finding the place where I'd gutted the rabbit.

Of course, there was no trace of entrails to mark the spot. Some meat eater—an owl, fox, opossum, or perhaps, a raccoon—would have found and eaten everything almost at once.

I got the feeling that if my knife was there I might not find it. The fence was long, maybe half a mile. Maybe it was the night. Things have a way of looking different at night. A flashlight can throw grotesque shadows. Perhaps I should wait for daylight.

I looked at my watch. Four-thirty. I could go back home, have breakfast, and then come back here. I sat down on the stone fence and put out the flashlight.

It was the darkest hour of the night, the time before dawn. It was also the most eerie time, the quietest time. By now, most of the night animals would be done foraging and looking for a place to hole up for the day. Night birds, too—crops full—would be back home in trees watching for the dawn.

Even Molly had stopped running, and I supposed she had gone back to her pups, perhaps to let them nurse for what little milk was left in her dugs . . . Perhaps I dozed, because it seemed that all of a sudden, there was a bright dagger of light thrusting up into the sky—a sharp blade of pink from the east where the sun was getting ready to rise on another day.

I rubbed my eyes, yawned, and stood up and stretched. Perhaps I was wrong. Maybe, there was only one knife. When the sheriff's deputies combed the woods looking for evidence, they could have found the knife I left there. That much of it was understandable. What I still couldn't understand—if it was my knife—is how Jake's blood got on it!

I walked a little way back into the woods where a small brook with clear, cold water came from a bubbling spring. I knelt, and bending my head, drank. Then I splashed water on my face.

The slash of pink had spread until the entire eastern half of the sky was tinted. The light was reaching down now through the branches and into the shadowy places beneath the brambles. It was bright enough to make a more thorough inspection of the stone fence.

I went slowly, stopping often to view a particular section of fence where it appeared the rocks might have recently been moved. Stones tend to discolor on the damp, bottom side. If I'd overturned any while digging out the rabbit, the discolored side would be facing up.

In a couple places, it appeared the rocks had been recently moved. I searched these areas thoroughly, but I kept having the feeling that I had not found the right place.

When I came to the eastern end of the fence, I sat down. I was disappointed. When I'd left my bed, I felt certain I would find my knife, that it would still be on the rock where I'd placed it.

Actually, it probably wasn't especially important. Because who would believe it if I told them there was a second knife? Who would believe I hadn't invented the story to direct suspicion toward someone else?

Still, if my knife was here, I wanted to find it. It would explain for me, if not for anybody else, why a knife exactly like mine was covered with Tabor's blood.

I was turning back to survey the west end of the stone fence when Molly came tail-wagging through the underbrush.

"Hungry, girl?" I asked.

She whined, and then out from among the trees, running and tumbling, came the five pups. They ganged around their mother tugging at her long, velvety ears, chewing on her strong-boned hound dog legs.

Molly scattered the pups with a few sharp nips and low growls. They converged on me, and one after another got a toothhold on my pants ends and tugged.

I let them play until they were tired and then went west again, searching for the place where I'd dug the rabbit out from the rocks.

The dogs trotted along. Molly stayed a discreet distance behind, but the pups were always getting underfoot. Together, we went all the way to the end of the fence, and again, I was unable to identify that part of the fence into which Panther had chased the rabbit.

By the time we started back, the sun was at its midmorning station in the sky, and I was getting hungry. The pups obviously were hungry, too, and when I stopped to rest and Molly stretched out near me in the grass, they ganged up at her side to try for what little milk might still be squeezed from her shrinking breasts. The trouble was, they had long, sharp, puppy teeth, and when no milk was forthcoming, they prodded poor Molly with their heads and paws and yanked with their demanding mouths at her tender teats.

One pup finally drew blood, and Molly whirled with a yelp of pain and sent the pups scattering in all directions. She lay down again, but each time they came back, she lashed out at them. Finally, she caught one pup by an ear and bit him hard. He went yelping and the others withdrew; so, perhaps it was then they really understood that their walking milk factory had finally run out of milk.

The bewildered pups lay for awhile just

looking at her. Then the largest of the litter picked up a stick and the rest of the little pack chased him for it. They went around and around—first one, and then another, the proud possessor of the stick —until all five dropped down in the grass exhausted.

I got up then and proceeded slowly along the edge of the woods. Molly trailed at my heels, and the five pups were strung out behind her. When I had retraced my steps and was almost to the eastern end of the stone fence, I sat down again.

It was like looking for a tiny pearl in a mountain of gravel. The dry autumn grass almost hid some of the stones, and vines had crawled out of the woods in many places to get their tendrils into crevices and build a spiderlike webbing over the fence.

The pups had revived and were tussling on a mound of earth freshly thrown up by a burrowing woodchuck. The chuck was probably sleeping, taking one of those long, long naps which precede hibernation.

Molly was satisfied to be left alone. She stretched at my feet. But the pups, not satisfied to merely romp, were taking turns entering the chuck's burrow. Each would go in a little way and then back out like a child tasting the spooky feeling of a cave.

I had about given up by then. If the knife

was somewhere along the stone fence, I was sure it would be quite by accident if I ever found it. I'd go home, get something to eat, and then bring food for the dogs.

Molly was looking gaunt. What with having suckled five pups, then running most of every night, I could see the latticework of her ribs through her sleek, black hide.

So I'd feed her, and pretty soon, I'd have to decide what must be done with her and the five pups, because they surely couldn't continue to live in the woods.

But that was something for some other time. First, there would be my trial. And then? I didn't want to think of it.

I got up and climbed over the stone fence to take Molly and the pups back to their brushpile. Molly came, but the pups did not follow. I whistled softly, but they didn't appear.

Now what, I thought, not without some irritation. I waited, and then I went back. One of them had what looked like a stick and the other four had followed him out into a stubble field.

They went around and around, farther and farther. I recrossed the stone fence and whistled again, but they ignored me. I looked down at Molly. She looked up at me.

"Pretty naughty," I said, and then I laughed in spite of myself.

The chase ended far out in the field and now the stick had been picked up by another one of the pups; he was coming back toward us as fast as his oversized paws would permit.

I expected I'd have to get the stick to end the game. I walked toward the pup who was leading the pack and when he went by, I bent over and swept him up into my arms.

"And now, the stick, please . . ." I started to say. Then something caught my eye. I let the pup go, leaned forward, and there in the gravel, at the entrance to the woodchuck's hole, was my knife! The pups, while playing, must have dug it up.

7

Dad called Mr. Benz to tell him about the second knife. I was standing so close to the phone I could hear the attorney.

"Well, it's an angle. Maybe we can make something of it. But we'll have to convince the jury that there were two knives . . . that we didn't plant the second one and make up the story."

"Think we ought to give the knife to the sheriff?" Dad asked.

"No, we'll keep it as a surprise exhibit. I'll pick it up and take it to a laboratory to get an analysis. How long was it lying out in the woods . . . you know . . . the usual stuff."

"Okay," Dad said, and hung up.

When he turned from the phone, he said to me, "If only you hadn't told the sheriff the knife they found was yours."

"But I thought it was mine," I said.

"Of course you did. It was the logical conclusion. You had to tell what you thought was the truth."

I couldn't help thinking then that if I'd lied, perhaps the sheriff and the district attorney wouldn't have been so certain I was the murderer, and they'd have continued their investigation. Perhaps then, they might even have found the real killer.

"Well, anyway," Dad said, starting toward the kitchen, "at least one part of the puzzle has been solved for us, even if nobody believes it." It was important that we knew the whole truth about the knives, even if no one else did.

Dad must have been thinking the same thing, because he said: "Maybe it's only a little thing, finding the knife. But it puts our house in order, like finding the last piece of a jigsaw puzzle under the carpet."

I nodded, but then added, "Except it doesn't bring us any closer to discovering who it was that really did it."

Dad rubbed his forehead with his hands and mused, "No it doesn't. And I wonder . . . I wonder who it could have been?"

I hesitated before answering, but finally, I said, "I don't know, but I can't get Bob Bacon off my mind."

Dad looked thoughtful. "It does look bad for him, doesn't it? Poking around down there like he is. But I've known Bob all my life. He's a bum. You've got to say it, because he drifts whichever way the wind blows. He's a bum all right, but an innocent sort of bum. I can't believe Bob Bacon could kill—not even an ant."

Everybody knew Bob Bacon, of course. Well almost everybody, anyway. He was a fixture in Coulee City. Other bums might come and go, but Bob had lived there all his life.

Some said he had never been too bright. When his father ran away and his mother died, he just sort of drifted down to Skid Row, to Water Street, and he'd been living out of garbage cans since.

You had to feel sorry for a guy like that. You had to be thankful that your own father hadn't run away and that your mother hadn't died, or you might have ended up on Skid Row yourself.

"I've got to feed those dogs," I said abruptly. "Molly hasn't any milk left, and those pups are driving her crazy."

"Well, when you do feed her, ask her who killed Jake Tabor." We both laughed, and I was amazed that I was still capable of laughter. It really wasn't so funny. I was sure Molly knew, and I also knew that unlocking her mind was impossible.

It was warm walking back down along the hedgerow to the woods, but I wasn't being fooled. Most of the birds had gone south, and most ducks had left the river. Winter was right around the corner, and when it came with zero cold and cutting winds, Black Haw Woods would be no place for Molly and her young pups.

Panther went with me, and when I got to the brushpile, Molly was lying in the sun in a dust-hole she'd dug for herself. The pups were resting too—scattered about on the ground like blackberries shaken from the vine.

They all greeted me with enthusiasm, but when I dumped out the food, they forgot all else in the rush to fill their shrinking bellies.

I made my getaway while they were still absorbed in satisfying their hunger. Instead of heading back home, however, I turned and walked toward the river. I came to the water where Deer Track Peninsula juts out and Bloodstone River winds around in an intricate oxbow. From this vantage point, I could see up and down the main stream for a considerable distance.

A flock of migrating bluebills got up with a wild rush of stubby wings when Panther went in belly-deep for a drink. He stood watching them, and then he looked back at me as if to say: "Well, we missed a good chance. If you'd brought your gun, I'd be retrieving a duck now." He drank.

There was only one boat on the river. It was too far away for me to recognize the man hunched over on the middle seat above three cane poles which jutted out over the water. But I didn't have to get closer to recognize the yellow boat. It was old Hughie (Big Fish) Frazer's. He fished all the time. It was the way he made his living, and the law closed its eyes when he sold fish (which was illegal) because everybody said it was better than having him on relief.

Reluctant to turn back, I followed the shoreline down to where Hughie was fishing. There were mink and fox tracks and I spooked several muskrats that had been busy adding yet a few more rushes to their domed huts.

When I came opposite to where Hughie was fishing, he waved, and I waved back. As soon as I sat on a big rock to watch, he wrapped up his poles, pulled anchor, and rowed over.

"Hi, Danny," he said, beaching the rowboat.

"Hi, Hughie," I greeted him. "How's fishing?"

For an answer, he held up a stringer. He had two northern pike which looked as though they'd weigh five pounds apiece, and three walleyed pike in about the two-pound class.

"Nice fish," I said.

"They bite in fall," he said. "It's the best time of the year."

"What you using?"

"Frogs. Never use nothing but frogs in fall. The fish expect frogs in fall. They know they're coming into the water to dive into the mud for winter."

It made sense.

"Say," Hughie asked, "what the heck's been going on around here?"

"Why, what do you mean?"

"Well, there's been more traffic along this river the past weeks than I've seen in a whole year."

I didn't say anything right away. Hughie dug out a package of cigar clippings and, spitting out the chew he had in his mouth, stuffed fresh tobacco into his cheek.

He was an old man. His face was the color and texture of an old horse harness that's been left lying in the sun, and his whiskery face and the hair which stuck out from beneath his brown, battered hat, were salted with gray.

As if remembering something, he asked, "They having any luck finding the real murderer?" Just like that. Like he knew that, of course, I didn't do it.

I shook my head. "They aren't looking," I said. "They're convinced I'm their man."

"Darn fools!" Hughie said.

I thought so, too, of course, but I couldn't help but wonder why Hughie did. He didn't know me that well. Or did he? He'd lived on the outskirts of Coulee City all his life. He'd probably been old when I was born. These old-timers could really surprise a fellow. It was almost as if they absorbed knowledge as an angleworm does oxygen, right through their skin.

Hughie spit, narrowed his eyes, and then asked, "You know where that hound dog, Molly, is?"

I was so taken aback by the abruptness of his question that, for a moment, I couldn't answer. When I did, I put him off with a question to gain time. "You mean the one Jake Tabor was looking for the day he was killed?"

Hughie chuckled. "Okay, you don't have to tell me. But all I got to say is that there's an awful lot of people seems interested in finding that dog."

"Like who?"

"How would I know?" Hughie said.

Panther had wandered off, and now we could hear him back in the marsh grass plowing through potholes. Every once in a while, a black duck or a mallard climbed skyward, quacking with consternation.

"That's a good dog you got," Hughie said, changing the subject.

I just nodded, and then asked the question

that was bothering me, "Recognize any of the people who have been nosing around?"

"Of course," Hughie said.

I waited, because I figured if he was going to
tell me, he would, and if he wasn't, he wouldn't.

Hughie came at it from an angle . . . "That
Molly must sure be one fine dog?" He made it a
question. I only nodded, so he continued, "Worth
maybe two thousand dollars?"

I nodded again. "Maybe more for the right
man."

"Ain't no dog's worth more than a hun-
dred," he said flatly, as if it was a fact, as if he dared
me to deny it.

From Hughie's point of view, that was cor-
rect. A hunter could probably kill as much game
with a one-hundred-dollar dog as he could with a
two-thousand-dollar one. But for a man who followed the field trials, the one dog in a thousand
with just that little extra something was worth
whatever a man could afford to pay.

I knew of one retriever like Panther who
had been sold for fifteen thousand dollars when he
was but two years old. Most hounds, however,
never went for anywhere near that kind of money
—although I'd heard of several selling for as much
as two thousand dollars.

There was a fanatical fringe of field trial fol-
lowers who would lie, beg, steal and maybe—just

maybe—even kill to get a dog that had struck their fancy.

Well, Molly was one of those expensive dogs, and I couldn't help wondering when next she'd run in a field trial and who would cast her on the trail of the coon.

Hughie had been talking, but I hadn't been listening until I heard Bob Bacon's name. Then I turned my attention back to him.

"I don't know what Bob would want with that dog," Hughie was saying, "unless it is to find her for Matt. The dog rightly belongs to Matt. It was his dad's, so now I suppose she is his."

Hughie was right. The dog did rightfully belong to Matt Tabor or maybe Jake's wife, although nobody knew where she was. That is, unless, of course, Jake had died with so many debts the dog would have to be sold to satisfy his creditors.

"I suppose now that Jake's dead," I said, "Bob is running favors for Matt."

"I wouldn't know," Hughie said. "I saw them together back in the marsh one afternoon. But then, like I said, the traffic has been heavy."

A thought struck me, but I put it out of my head. A son could never kill his own father. Not that Jake wouldn't have given Matt a reason to kill him. There was no end to the list of men whom Jake had abused. He had been like a hornet—once aroused, he stung anybody who got in the way.

"Clyde Barnes, Dell James, Ted Feldman
. . . a lot of the field trial crowd have been hunting
the shore," Hughie continued. "In Feldman's case,
maybe he's trying to protect his investment."

I didn't know what Hughie meant, so I
asked him.

"Well, Jake was lock, stock, and barrel in
debt to Feldman. Some say Feldman was waiting
for the day he could foreclose and move Molly and
all Jake's hounds over to his place."

It was amazing the things Hughie seemed to
know, but I couldn't be sure whether they were all
facts or some things an old fisherman had dreamed
up.

"But then," Hughie went on, "even his wife
would have reason enough to kill him. He beat her
something terrible."

It was then I realized that Hughie was actually listing for me everyone he knew who might,
during a desperate moment, jump on Jake's back
and put a knife in his neck.

Trouble was, most of the suspects, although
they might want to see Jake dead, could never have
accomplished the killing themselves. Bob Bacon,
like Dad had said, was too timid. Mrs. Tabor
wasn't living in Coulee City. Ted Feldman, grocer
and owner of the feed store, was too respectable to
risk it. And so it went with all the others. When it
was all sifted down there was only Matt!

8 When I left Hughie, he handed me two walleyed pike. "A present for your mother," he said. "She's always been nice to me."

Once again, I couldn't help but be surprised. I knew that my mother was acquainted with Hughie, but who in Coulee City didn't know Hughie? I would never have guessed, however, that their paths had crossed and that she had made such a favorable impression on him.

"Thanks," I said. "Thanks. My mother will be happy with the fish. She likes fish."

"I know," Hughie said, standing to shove off.

I cut a forked branch and strung the fish on it, and then waving to Hughie, cut back up along the shore of Deer Track Peninsula and headed for Black Haw Woods.

The school bus had just stopped down at the end of our road when I walked into the yard with Panther. My two brothers, Jack and Jim, got off and came running. Both were shouting, "Danny, can we come to your trial? Can we?"

My mother must have heard them, because she appeared at the kitchen door. "Get right in here now," she admonished the boys, "and leave Danny alone." I handed her the fish and told her Hughie had sent them.

"Oh, isn't that nice," she said. "And how is he?"

"Fine," I said, "just fine . . . fishing as usual."

The boys went reluctantly into the house to change clothes so they might feed the chickens and pigs. I went to the barn and began feeding the cows.

Sometimes I seemed to forget about the trial. I don't know how I did it. Unless it was because now I was concentrating so hard on trying to come up with some answers—answers which eluded me like owls in the shadowy aisles of a nighttime woods.

The boys' questions were a reminder that the trial was only a week away, and I still didn't know how Mr. Benz was going to defend me or what he intended doing.

So far, during our infrequent discussions, he listed names of townspeople who were going to testify as to my good character, but he had found no way to refute the damaging accusations of Bob Bacon and Matt Tabor.

Now that we knew there had been two knives, we could play that for all it was worth. Maybe, just maybe, the jury would buy it.

But what else? I had been along the edge of Black Haw Woods the day it happened, and I had admitted it. Then I had said mistakenly that the knife was mine, and . . .

I tried to put it from my mind. Instead, I concentrated on trying to find a reason why so many people should be interested in finding Molly —even though she might be worth two thousand dollars. What could they gain? What good would it do them?

I was pouring the last pail of milk into the cooling vat when the answer came to me. It hit me like a lance of sunshine coming through the crack of a corncrib to light up a dusty corner.

They weren't looking for Molly! They were looking for the pups! Everybody knew she'd been about ready to whelp the day she disappeared. They could pick up the pups, leave Molly behind, and even if someone at sometime guessed that they

were the pups of Jake Tabor's dog, it could never
be proved.

I wondered why I hadn't thought about it
before. Molly's pups would make great field trial
prospects. Whoever found them would have no
trouble in signing some other bitch's name to the
registration application. It's incredible, I thought,
how easy it would all be, and I had failed to see
the obvious even when it was right in front of my
nose.

Someone was sure to find the pups now that
they spent most of their days roaming the woods in
the vicinity of the lair.

Still, it would be stealing. The pups belonged to the Tabors. Any right-minded man
would know that. I reassured myself that not all
men were honest. There were some who weren't
above stealing—or killing, for that matter.

I didn't get down to Black Haw Woods the
next day or the day after that. I spent each day in
Coulee City in Mr. Benz's office while we went
over again and again the meager evidence we might
present in my defense.

The laboratory analysis of the knife came
back. The bloodstains, as I knew, were not of
human blood. The analysis further showed that the
knife had been exposed to the elements for a considerable length of time.

Of course, Attorney Benz kept insisting,

"The prosecution is going to maintain we are lying, that there was really but one knife, and that we deliberately put bloodstains on a second knife."

On the morning of the third day, Dad got a call from George Reims, our neighbor to the east. A dog had killed one of his sheep, and he wondered if we had been having any raids on our livestock or poultry.

Dad, of course, told him we hadn't. When he hung up, he came out into the kitchen to tell me about it. Then he said, "George is going to set traps, and you know who is going to get caught."

So it had been a mistake to let Molly and her pups forage for themselves for two days and two nights. I should have fed them.

"Maybe you'd better go down right now and feed them before Molly gets into more trouble," Dad said.

I started through the kitchen door, and he called me back. "Maybe, better yet . . ." He hesitated. I waited. Then he went on, "Maybe better if you'd wait until tonight and then just bring the dogs up here and we'll call Matt Tabor to come and get them."

I went back into the kitchen then and sat down. I looked at Dad, but didn't say anything. Finally, he broke the silence and said, "I know it is going to look bad. I know people are going to think you had the dog and were hiding her all along. But, what else?"

He was right. What else? So I spent the afternoon changing oil in the tractor and the car and greasing them. Twice during the late hours of the day I thought I heard shotgun blasts from the direction of Black Haw Woods, but decided the sound was from hunters' guns along Bloodstone River.

After chores that night, I got a length of rope from the machine shed, and when it was dark, locked Panther in the barn. I also put a small amount of dog food in a bran sack in case Molly was reluctant and, snapping on a flashlight, started out.

Above me, stars shone, but the sky to the west was black; I was sure the clouds were bringing snow. I crossed the garden and my light picked out the frozen yellow cucumbers, the red tomatoes, rotting on the ground, and pumpkins yellow as butter. When I came to the hedgerow I put out the light and followed it.

At the edge of Black Haw Woods, I paused to listen. I didn't want to run into anyone. When there was nothing to see or hear, I moved into the woods, walking carefully. Near the brushpile I stood to listen again. When I resumed walking, the first few flakes of snow began to filter through the shadowy, bare branches of the trees.

I came to the edge of the small clearing the dogs and I had trampled in the woods and took the light from my pocket. I shone it on the pile of

85

brush beneath which the dogs had their lair. But there were no dogs in sight. I waited a few moments and then whistled softly.

There was no excited charge of puppies as I had been expecting. There was nothing. I whistled softly again. When no dogs showed themselves, I went forward and standing in front of the brushpile called, "Molly, Molly."

I shone my light into her den. She was gone. The pups were gone. I circled around and around the brushpile in ever-widening circles. There was no sign of them so I came back.

I stood at the brushpile and stared at the ground as if there I might find an explanation for their disappearance. Then I saw the leg of a sheep. I picked it up. It had been gnawed clean of flesh, and there was wool scattered on the ground—wool which looked like the snow which was beginning to cover the ground.

I dumped out the food—just in case—then I turned away and walked through the now heavily falling snow.

The snow seemed to change everything. The yard lights were on, and
by the time I got back to the house,
it had softened even the harsh fence

9

wires into looking like white cottony ropes. I stood
in the yard as though before the home of a
stranger. Gone were all the sharp roof lines, the
bare branches above them. Gone were the black,
frozen tracks in the muddy yard. Gone were the
gaunt shapes of tractor, wagon, and reaper and in
their stead stood softly molded, almost shadowy
sculptures, outlined in the purest white.

For a moment, I had the feeling that ghosts

had come in my absence to shroud our utilitarian little world with a filmy gauze from some fairyland. And how easily it had been accomplished. In minutes, the rough edges had been softened. In minutes, the grim sheds had been camouflaged. Like magic, all the straggling vines, sparse grasses, tangled weeds were woven into delicate webs of fine, white lace.

Dad, coming through the kitchen door, broke the spell. He came over to where I was standing and said, "So you changed your mind. About bringing her in, I mean."

I brushed at the snow on my forehead and said, "No, Dad, she was gone, and so were the pups."

"You think someone found her?"

"I don't know. But there was the leg of a sheep near the den, so she must be the killer."

"About that I never had any doubts," Dad said.

"Anyhow," I tried to be light-hearted about it, "that takes me off the hook. Now they won't know that I was feeding her. They won't be able to say I was hiding her down there."

"That's important," Dad said.

I guess it was important, because how would it look if they discovered I knew all along where the dog was, and that I'd been feeding her? They'd say, of course, that I had been hiding her.

It snowed all night. I slept poorly, partly because I had one ear tuned to hear if Molly might bay. I didn't hear her. Still, I lay listening, but all sounds were muffled as if the noisy world had been packed in cotton.

The next morning I was up early, and right after chores, I put a sandwich in the pocket of my sheepskin-lined jacket, and leaving Panther behind, headed back to Black Haw Woods.

It was slow going. In the open stretches, the snow was nearly knee-deep. I should have worn snowshoes, but they were clumsy things to maneuver in a woods so filled with underbrush.

When I got to the brushpile, I circled. Beneath the trees, the snow was not as deep as out in the open. I moved faster in ever-widening circles—crossing deer tracks, the spoor of two hunting foxes, the birdlike tracks of several white-footed mice, the wing marks of an owl or crow—but no dog tracks.

I went all the way to Bloodstone River which wound its way like a blue-black serpent through the snow-covered marshes. Then I brushed the snow from a huge rock and sat down.

It was reasonably safe to say Molly was not in the woods or I'd have crossed her trail. Either something had frightened Molly and she had fled with the pups for some more distant hideout, or someone had found and taken her in.

In a way, I hoped she had been found. Survival in the snow would be a problem. Even the wild ones—foxes, raccoons, and mink—might find hunting hard.

I ate my sandwich and debated with myself what my next move should be. To the north, along the river, was a sharp outcropping of bluffs. To the south, the land went flat, and the river moved through nearly impenetrable swamps.

Perhaps, I thought, I should look around the George Reims farm. Molly might have headed in that direction, although it was unlikely she would linger. The place was intensively farmed and provided scant cover.

Anyway, I headed east and north. Shortly, I broke out of the marsh and after passing through a fringe of trees, stood where I could look all the way across the Reims place, even beyond their buildings which stood on a slight rise.

I stayed to the edge of the fields until I came to a trampled area which I knew at once was baited to catch a sheepkiller. What was left of the sheep carcass had been wired to a stone so an animal might not drag it away, and, when I moved closer, I could make out the location of four steel traps hidden in the snow.

They were large traps, number four jumps. They were large and strong enough to easily break a leg on a dog the size of Molly.

90

For a moment, I was tempted to step into the bait circle and spring the traps. I thought better of it, however, because one of the Reims boys would be sure to track me; that would mean more trouble. So I turned and drifted toward home.

Mr. Benz's car was in the yard so I went right in. He had heard about the sheep killing and the rumors that Molly might be the culprit.

"Makes sense," he said. "Everybody knows that dog's gotta be down there somewhere."

So I told him. I admitted that we had known all along that Molly was in the woods. Dad helped me and, between us, we gave him all the details, even down to finding the sheep's leg at the lair and now the disappearance of Molly and her pups.

To say he was surprised is putting it mildly. His face was white when we finished. When he could talk he said, "Don't look for her! Stay out of the woods! If anyone even suspects you've been hiding her, your goose is cooked."

"But we haven't been hiding the dog," I interrupted.

"What do you call it then?"

"She was hiding herself. We were merely feeding her," I said.

"A technicality. Without your help, she'd never have made it. She'd have had to come out for food. Whether you admit it or not, you were hiding her. If anyone finds out . . ." He didn't finish, just raised his hands and shook his head.

Dad placated him. "The dog is gone," he said, "so there's no point in worrying about it any longer. The pups are gone, too. Perhaps someone found them."

Mr. Benz got up to go. The color which had drained from his face was returning. "Just don't go down there," he said. "Goodness knows, we've got enough trouble as it is without adding to it."

He was right . . . we did have enough trouble. But I couldn't feel sorry for what I had done. In fact, I would have felt much worse, knowing the dog was down there, if I hadn't at least made an effort to feed her and the pups.

Maybe Mr. Benz was reading my mind, because he stopped at the door to say, "I know how you felt, but you should have stayed away. You should have let word get around about her being there. Someone else could have picked her up and you wouldn't have gotten involved."

He went out, and I turned to Dad. "What do you think?" I asked.

"About what?"

"About where Molly is?"

"I don't know. It's a mystery. If someone has picked her up, surely we'd have heard by now."

"But someone must have."

"Why? Do you think someone found her?"

"I went all through the woods. I followed the river as far as the bluffs. I went over to Reims' place. There were no tracks, not one dog track."

"Maybe she went farther."

"With pups?"

"They were big enough to travel."

When I went to bed that night, I fell instantly asleep. Perhaps it was nervous exhaustion because, when I awakened sometime during the early morning hours, my joints ached as they sometimes did after a long winter day in the woods sawing trees.

Something awakened me—of that I was sure—because when I opened my eyes, I was already up on an elbow listening. But I could hear nothing.

I got up and went quietly as possible to the window, but no matter how carefully I walked, the old floor boards creaked and the sound startled me even though I'd heard them creak a thousand times before.

There was a nearly full moon and the snow glistened as if sprinkled with diamonds. Sinking to the floor, I put my arms on the window sill and rested my chin on them. Outside, nothing moved. The moon cast shadows into the tracks which crisscrossed the yard, and near the garden gate a snowman my brothers had made stared up at me with its black, coal eyes.

Perhaps I fell asleep sitting there with my chin on my folded arms. I don't know, but I was suddenly startled by a sharp report and, for a moment, I thought it was gunfire. When I could collect myself, I realized it was only the old house protesting and perhaps complaining about the deep cold which was putting its invisible hands to making ice.

The cold seeped beneath the window frame, and I shivered. Now there would be no return to the intermittent days of warm weather. Winter was truly settling in, and the perilous days were here for the wild ones—including Molly and her pups—if they were still out there where the snow was building a hard crust to protect seedlings.

I lifted my head, thinking to get back beneath the warm covers, when something stopped me. It couldn't be, I thought—not Molly—because what coon would be abroad? Although, there could be coons moving, as they never truly hibernate. They only nap and then come down out of their tree dens, to forage for food along the open creeks or down where swift rivers stay the formation of ice.

Still, I couldn't believe I had heard the dog and figured maybe my mind was playing tricks on me. I wanted to believe that Molly had not been picked up, that she was still down there somewhere.

There was nothing though, nothing to hear

no matter how I strained forward, my forehead pressing against the cold window pane. I got up then and turned to go back to bed when once again something stopped me.

That is Molly, I thought. But in the same moment that I thought I heard her, the sound eluded me, and there was nothing to break the stillness.

I didn't go back to bed, mainly because I was sure I couldn't sleep. Instead, I opened the window and then unhinged and braced the storm window.

Cold air rushed into the room, and my breath was suddenly white—the plume of it put a frosty pattern on the pane of the tilted storm window. I dropped to a sitting position to listen.

Then I heard it—far off, and thin, and brittle as the night air itself—unmistakably, the voice of Molly coursing along whatever trail the coon had laid. It was incredible that she should hunt when now, hungry and in deep snow, the chase could bring her nothing but pain. Still, that was her destiny, to trail forever through all the years of her life.

When I was sure it was Molly keening from far across the fields, I wanted to dress at once, strap on snowshoes, and go to her . . . Perhaps I might have, except, once again, Dad appeared in my doorway.

"Is it her?" he asked.

I nodded, and then, when I realized that perhaps in the dark he might not be able to see me, I said, "It's Molly."

"I thought so. For the last hour, I kept thinking I heard her. Except I couldn't believe it."

"Neither could I."

"Where do you think she is?" he asked.

"Among the bluffs. It's the only place. Three small creeks come down to the river there. Coons would be working them."

"Think she's got the pups with her?"

"Who knows," I said. "Perhaps someone picked them up and that's what frightened her off."

"Could be."

We were both silent then; now, Molly's voice came more clearly through the window. Distance and the extreme cold, however, gave it an unusual timbre.

"Think she sounds sick?" I asked, fearful suddenly that something had happened to her.

"No," Dad said, "it's the cold, and the distance, and the bluffs. All things sound different among the bluffs."

I knew that. The abrupt hills seemed to squeeze sound, to thin it out. Sitting there in the icy air which was coming through the window, I thought it sounded eerie, ghostly—a faraway siren sounding like a woman wailing.

96

"Maybe I ought to go down there?" I made it a question.

"At night? In the cold?"

"But it's as bright as day," I said, gesturing toward the shimmering fields.

"It can wait," Dad said. "She'll still be there when it's daylight. Then you can track her. Your mother would be upset if you went now. She feels bad enough as it is."

Actually, I should have stayed away—but I couldn't let the dog starve. But Dad was right. If anything could be done, I could do it tomorrow as well as tonight.

"I'm freezing," Dad said. "I'm going to bed. Close the window. Get some sleep. Likely you'll have a big day tomorrow."

10 I was finishing a hasty breakfast under the worried eye of my mother, when I heard a car come into the yard. I went to a window and looked out. It was Mr. Benz. I thought about slipping out a side door before he came in, because I was sure when he heard about the dog he would argue that I should stay away from her . . . He caught me as I was getting my hat, jacket, and gloves from the entryway.

"Good morning," I said, rather formally.

"Good and cold," he said, rubbing his hands together briskly.

Dad, who obviously had heard the car, too, came up from the barn, and while he ushered Mr. Benz into the kitchen, I ducked out the back door.

My snowshoes were in the machine shed, and I went to get them. Panther trailed along but, once again, I took him to the barn and locked him up. I was coming back up across the yard with my snowshoes over one shoulder when my mother came out wrapped in a shawl and handed me a sandwich.

"Just be careful," she said.

"I will, Mother, I will," I said as I bent to strap on the snowshoes.

She was shivering, but she didn't go back into the house. I gave her a quick kiss on the cheek, and said, "Don't worry, Mother."

I was just to the garden gate when Mr. Benz came out and shouted to me, "You can't go down there. What are you thinking of?"

My dad was right behind Mr. Benz, and I heard him say, "No matter what, we can't knowingly let that dog starve."

I didn't bother to turn around. But as I broke snow away in front of the gate so I could open it, I heard Mr. Benz say, "————, it's only three days until the trial. What's he thinking of? Doesn't he care if he goes to prison!"

The cold had put just enough crust on the snow to make moving at a reasonable pace comfortable. I bypassed Black Haw Woods and moved in a direct line toward the bluffs. They lifted like small, flat-topped mountains covered mainly with hickory, hard maple, and scattered groves of juniper.

Fences gave me the most trouble. A few were strung loose enough to be crossed without removing my snowshoes, but most had tight wires spaced so close I had to stop, take off the snowshoes, cross, and put them on again.

It took me until nearly noon to get to the first creek at the base of the first bluff. I took off my snowshoes and fastened them to my back to make the ascent more certain with the sure footing of boots.

It was a rare morning. The crisp, cold, moonlit night had turned into a blue day of brilliant sunshine. At the foot of the bluffs, the snow cover was largely unmarked. I started my ascent slowly. If Molly was here, I reasoned, she'd likely be in one of the valleys which came narrowly between the hills.

Halfway up the first slope, I turned to look back. The view was breathtaking. From an outcropping of rock, I could look between the trees down upon the endless succession of blinding, white fields cut neatly with the straight lines of fences and their shadows in the snow.

Along the horizon stood the buildings of the George Reims farm looking like little doll buildings set down by some child in a field of cotton batting spread around in play to resemble snow.

The air was pure, and cold, and exhilarating. I filled my lungs with it, forgetting that within three days I would be in court in Coulee City answering to a charge of murder. I forgot about my concerned father, my worried mother. I even forgot why I had come to these hills, such was the intoxication of the moment—the sharp, clear, brilliant moment.

Of course, the good feeling didn't last. The moment of exhilaration passed, and I turned and started up again. In some places, the slope was so steep I climbed from tree to tree. Although I was young and strong, I had to rest often. By the time I topped out, reached the summit, I was breathing heavily; despite the cold, I was perspiring.

The top of the bluff was flat and relatively smooth. I crossed it and, in a small clearing, looked down into the next valley where Trout Creek writhed like a long, black snake.

So far, there hadn't been any dog tracks. A few deer had left their prints, and a single fox had come down the hill, probably heading for some meadow to dig down for mice.

Going downhill was easier, however, somewhat more precarious. Again, I moved from tree to tree because the slope had been windswept and was slippery.

The valley, of course, had been the wind's

dumping ground, and here, the snow was piled high. I went straight to the creek, and padding out a place along the bank, knelt down for a drink of the icy water.

When I got up, I strapped on my snowshoes and followed the water up to where I knew the spring bubbled. The creek narrowed and, at last, I came to its source, a welter of boiling springs.

Here, I found coon tracks. Two animals had been poking in the mud for frogs and crayfish— that they had been successful was evident by spots of blood in the snow and the bright blue and orange shell casings and pincers. But there were no dog tracks. I retraced my steps.

There was nothing to do then but to assault the next bluff. I took off my snowshoes for the climb, and, this time, I went more slowly. When I reached the top, I was puffing; but from where I stood, I could see down on Bloodstone River; and I couldn't help thinking that the view itself was worth the climb.

The river, for the most part, was frozen and white. At intervals, however, there were open rapids—dark wounds on a winding, white snake.

But I couldn't waste time enjoying the scenery, so I crossed the top of the bluff and looked down into the next valley. Here, another stream, Boiling Water Creek, marked the valley floor.

I started down at once. Even before coming

out onto the narrow valley floor, I began to notice an abundance of wild game signs. There were ruffed grouse tracks. A weasel had loped along, inspecting hollows of logs and trees. Two coons had gone by. There were squirrel and rabbit tracks. So it probably was a rich valley.

When I came to the creek, I again knelt to strap on snowshoes. This time, however, instead of moving upstream, I followed the creek down in the direction of the river.

I don't know how far from the flat marshes I was when, among a welter of cottontail and snowshoe hare tracks, I saw the imprint of a dog's paw. I knelt to examine it. There was no mistaking it. Too large to be the paw print of a fox, I knew it had to be that of a large dog because the bluffs were too far south to hold coyotes.

I got up and proceeded down the gentle slope. It was not easy walking. White cedars grew in the valley, and they were askew, like bronze darts hurled carelessly to the ground by some gigantic hand.

I suppose I went a hundred yards when I saw more dog tracks, and then, a little farther down, there was a padded trail along the creek where Molly must have run often.

At one point, I found blood spots in the snow. My guess was that she had probably found and retrieved a dead trout from the creek.

103

Here in the wilderness, her breeding and training were against her. While she might quickly kill such a domestic animal as a sheep, she had been punished for running any wild creatures other than raccoons. Because it would have been such a serious sin to chase rabbits and hares, she would never have been able to bring herself to do it. I wondered how she had survived, and how she had been able to bring her pups through.

I'd walked nearly another half mile, and there the banks of the creek were padded smooth and hard by her paws and the pups' along a well-defined trail which went up to the side of the next bluff.

I felt better. The pups were still with her. Obviously, she had been bringing them down the slope to the creek, perhaps to drink. The way was clear for me to follow the trail they had made; sooner or later, I'd find them.

Once again, I took off my snowshoes and started up. Halfway to the top, I found the gut pile from a deer some hunter had killed. Picked over by the ravens, crows, and other forest meat eaters, Molly and her pups had taken what was left. It hadn't been much, and I could see where they'd sprawled in the snow to gnaw on what was left of the intestines, stomach lining, and the lungs of the deer.

The trail was steep and I had to rest often. I

knelt, sometimes, to peer beneath the brush in the hope that I would get a glimpse of them. Sometimes, I saw hares; once, I saw a porcupine lumbering along, and the sight of it increased my fear for the safety of the little pack. If they caught a porcupine on the ground and attacked it, they might come away with so many quills in their muzzles that, even after finding food, they would not have been able to eat it.

I was near the top and resting on a log when I got what I thought was my first glimpse of the dog. It was a fleeting hint of black and tan in the underbrush, and if it was Molly, she was avoiding me.

At once, I whistled softly, trying to make myself sound inviting. When no dogs showed, I tried again. But it was no use. If she or the pups heard me, they weren't about to accept my invitation.

I got up then and started to climb. At some points, the trail was so steep I had to brace from tree to tree to keep from sliding back down. Within sight of the top, I stopped to rest again; this time, I got a good look at Molly scooting through the brush.

I was on my feet at once, clambering over rock outcroppings and brush. I stayed close enough then to see her pop into the narrow mouth of a dark cave in the side of the bluff.

105

I sat down puffing from exertion, and, when I could breathe, I tried to whistle her out. Twice she came to the entrance so I could see her eyes glowing in the gloom of the cave.

I was completely confused. Overnight, it seemed, Molly had changed from a trusting, loving hound into a wild animal. I couldn't believe it. Dogs just didn't change like that. Perhaps, over a period of time, having no contact with man, they might revert to wilderness ways, but not in a matter of days.

When it became obvious that I couldn't whistle Molly out of the cave, I went the rest of the way up the slope to see if I might crawl in and drag her out. But the opening was too narrow.

I went back down a little way to wait. If I'd only thought to bring along food . . . I was sure I might have enticed her out into the open.

The sun made its noontime swing and started its westward slide. I took out the sandwich my mother had made for me, and put half of it close enough to the cave so the dogs might smell it. Then I went back to the log and sat to eat the other half.

Instead of Molly succumbing to the temptation of roast beef on rye, it turned out that the pups were the ones who couldn't resist the tantalizing odor.

They showed themselves tentatively at first,

like young mice peering up out of a nest to see if it was safe to make a seed-searching trip. I whistled low and soft, trying to calm whatever fears might have been implanted in their little heads.

Finally, all five had their heads out, like a picture—with the doorway of the cave as a frame. But it wasn't a pretty picture. The pups looked thin and sick. Their dark eyes looked almost cavernous and seemed sunk into the protruding bones of their heads. Their muzzles were stained with tears and their noses were leaking fluid. They were slowly starving; there was no doubt in my mind. Without help, they certainly would die.

The smell of meat was finally too much. They made a concerted rush for the half of sandwich, and it disappeared. Molly came out then. She rushed among the pups snapping, snarling. For a few moments, in their search for food, they ignored her. Then her threats got through to them, and turning and tumbling, one over the other, they retreated to the cave. Not relenting, Molly pursued, and they jostled each other to be the first to get inside beyond the sharp teeth of their angry mother.

It was a strange scene, so utterly different from the idyllic family life they had enjoyed while quartered in the lair beneath the brushpile. Seeing the family now, and seeing them then, was like seeing two dog packs having no relationship to each other.

Down below and far away in Black Haw Woods, they had been frolicking, easygoing, lovable hound dogs. Here, they were wild animals hiding in a dark cave, desperate for food, fearful, it seemed, for their lives.

I knew why! I knew in the instant that Molly turned away from me while she was driving the pups back. It was all there to read in the red wound along her shoulder, in the red streaks along the lattice-work of her ribs where the buckshot had raked her.

Molly had been shot. Perhaps twice. Maybe even three times. She had been shot and probably pursued, and it was likely that she and the pups had been hunted and hounded until, at last, they had been forced to flee the confines of Black Haw Woods, to take to the high hills, and to run like desperate, wild, hunted animals out ahead of the guns.

It was obvious. Molly's gods had betrayed her. Man, whom she had trusted more even than one of her own kind, had turned on her—blasted her with stinging, hot pellets of lead, shouted while driving her wildly through the woods, stayed on her trail across the fields—and had given her no surcease until she had taken the pups into these bluffs, these steep ravines, to this cave on the side of the little mountain.

It was a sad journey back for me. My own troubles—the prospect of jail—seemed somehow insignificant. Perhaps we had both been betrayed, **11** but, at least, I could understand. I was capable of making distinctions, sorting good men from bad.

The yard lights were on, but the moon hadn't yet risen when I finally came through the garden gate. I headed straight toward the kitchen door and then was brought up short by the sight of Mr. Benz's car down on the drive.

I didn't want an argument with the attorney. I was going back, regardless, so I could see no point in trying to explain to him why I thought it was the right thing to do—the *only* thing to do.

I had to eat something, and I had to let my parents know that I was back and safe.

First, I went to the feed shed and took down a fifty-pound sack of niblets. Then with reins from a couple of bridles, I strapped the sack so I could mount and carry it on my back. For good measure, and just in case she let me get close enough, I also coiled a long length of rope on the sack, and leaving all in readiness, went to the house.

My mother heard me at the door and was out in the entryway when I came in. I let her put her arms around me, and then I preceded her into the kitchen.

Mr. Benz arose. "Well, it's about time," he said. "Anybody see you down there?"

I didn't answer him, but looking over at my father said, "She's down there. In the bluffs. Somebody shot her. She won't let me get near."

"I know," my father said. "George Reims called. He took a posse through the woods. He said they hit her several times, that he was sure she had crawled away to die somewhere."

Mr. Benz tried to interrupt, but we both ignored him. "Well, she isn't dead," I said, "but if we don't get food out to them soon, they will be."

"Are the pups with her?"

110

I nodded. "And they are just as wild as she is."

"It happens," Dad said. "In all animals, even a docile cow, there's a pretty thin line between their wild past and their recent years of association with man."

When Dad finished talking he got up. Mr. Benz arose, too, and shaking a finger at me said, "All I've got to say is that you've got to stay away from that dog! Don't you understand the predicament you'd be in if someone discovered you were hiding that animal?"

From one point of view, of course, he was right. Still I couldn't resist the temptation to say, "Don't you realize the predicament Molly and her pups are in? Don't you understand that if I don't feed them, they are going to starve to death?"

Mr. Benz threw up his hands. It seemed as if he was always throwing up his hands. *"But they are only dogs!"* He put special emphasis on the word "dogs."

That sort of clinched it for me, and if the time for trial wasn't so close, I'd have asked Dad to get another lawyer. It confirmed the feeling I had about the man—an uneasiness which had made it difficult to view him as a friend.

Dad, of course, had hired him. He was the great-grandson of the man who had first handled our—the Stuarts'—affairs when my great-grandfather had homesteaded the land which now comprised our farm.

Over the years, there had been few legal problems for any of the Stuarts, but when there had been—mortgage, soil bank loans, tax questions—they had always gone to the Benzes because our first lawyer had been a Benz.

I'm afraid there would have been more argument, and it might have become heated now that I knew how Mr. Benz felt, but my mother stepped in and said, "That's enough of that for now. You haven't eaten. Go wash your hands, and I'll put on some food."

Mr. Benz and my father might have stayed right at the kitchen table while I ate, and the discussion might have continued, but my mother very forcibly told them to go into the living room to talk, "So the boy can eat in peace."

I never thought it was in my mother. She had been so withdrawn and moody since the charge of murder had been made against me that I never considered she might also be someone to lean on, to gather strength from.

When the two men went into the other room, she dished up pork chops, potatoes, and peas. I never knew how hungry I was until I smelled the food.

Mother sat across from me. She didn't say anything until my first hunger had been satisfied.

112

Then she asked, "You going back tonight?" When I nodded, she asked, "Do you think it is safe?"

"It's safe all right," I assured her. "There'll be a full moon. It'll be like daylight with all that snow on the ground."

"But what if you fall off a bluff? How'd we know? How'd we ever find you?"

"I won't fall, Mother. I won't."

I expected more objections, but there weren't any. She seemed stronger, and now that I think of it, we all seemed stronger. After the first shock had worn off, we had all gradually seemed to gather courage, perhaps one from the other, even though the odds seemed against us.

To change the subject, because I didn't want to further worry my mother about my proposed night trip back to the bluffs, I asked her how come Hughie Frazer knew her well enough to send along a gift of fish.

To my surprise, she blushed, and then lowering her head, laughed softly like a self-conscious little girl. I waited. When she looked back up at me, there was the hint of flirtatiousness in her eyes, or maybe I only thought there was. Then she said, "Would you believe it if I told you Hughie was once sweet on me?"

Hughie and my mother? Unbelievable!

She explained. "It was before I met your father. Hughie was much older but very respectable,

113

and we met at a church picnic down at the river picnic grounds. I even went with him for awhile and then your dad came along . . ." She hesitated, then slowly and deliberately she went on, "Well, after that, Hughie just seemed to lose interest in work, and pretty soon, he became what he is today, a man on the river fishing and, I suppose, just waiting out his time."

I didn't say anything for a minute, and then I felt compelled to say, "I can't help feeling sorry for Hughie."

She nodded. "I do, too. But it was a long time ago. Those things just happen, and when they do, there isn't much can be done about them."

I pushed my plate aside. We could hear my dad and the attorney in the front room. Sometimes, their voices were raised as though in argument. Sometimes, they talked in hushed tones. I was glad I didn't have to be a part of it. Mostly, I suppose I felt that no amount of talking could change anything.

Perhaps what I was thinking showed on my face, because my mother reached over and put her hand over mine. Just for a moment then, I wanted to cry. But I made myself rigid, gently pulled my hand away, and stood up.

"I have to get going," I said. "It's a long way. A long hike."

"Dress warm," Mother said. "The radio predicts it will go down to ten below tonight."

"I'll be moving all the time. I'll be warm," I assured her. Only then did her composure crack just a little, and I thought I saw tears standing in her eyes. "Don't worry," I said. "It'll be all right. I'll be careful. It's just a long walk, nothing more."

She smiled and said, "Okay, Danny, I won't worry. You're big enough now to take care of yourself."

I called in to Dad that I was going, and he and Mr. Benz came out into the kitchen. I could see the attorney was angry.

"You're a fool," he said. "I've got a good notion to withdraw from the case. If my great-grandfather hadn't been your great-grandfather's attorney, I'm sure I would. You haven't got a case to begin with, and you're jeopardizing what little chance you do have by such darn fool antics as feeding a stray dog and piling up more evidence against yourself."

What he said made my dad angry. I could see red at his collar line. He turned on the attorney. "We don't let animals starve," he said. "Not any animals. Not ours. Not someone else's. Not strays. If an animal is starving, we feed it!"

It wasn't what he said, but the way he said it that shut Mr. Benz up. It was the second surprise of the night for me. Not that I didn't know about Dad's temper, but what I hadn't known was that he could keep it so controlled that it was like a biting ax making sharp cuts without sending a lot of unnecessary splinters flying through the air.

All through supper, my two brothers had been upstairs, undoubtedly sent there by Mother when Mr. Benz came to talk. By now, they had crept down and were peering around the door, watching with wide eyes. I winked at them, and they grinned. Then I went for my jacket and said, "I have to get going."

Putting on my clothes, I went out. Mr. Benz followed, and I heard the door close. The moon had risen, and, standing there in its bright light, he looked at me. Finally, he said, "Be careful, boy. I can't approve of what you're doing. But just don't do anything foolish." Then he went to his car, and I went to the shed to get the bag of food and the rope.

I got into the pack straps I had fashioned, let the load settle onto the small of my back so it wasn't pulling at my shoulders; then, carrying my snowshoes, I started off across the yard.

The first mile was easy. Swinging rhythmically along on my snowshoes, I crossed field after field. Soon Black Haw Woods loomed darkly to my left and, in the distance, straight ahead, I saw the first faint outlines of the bluffs. I knew it was cold because my breath was freezing on my jacket collar, but I didn't feel it. Instead, I was lifted up, exhilarated by the white moonlight on the clean, white snow and by the feel of my muscles stretching and relaxing like well-oiled parts of a strong machine.

I went past the George Reims farm, dim in the distance, and the bluffs out ahead began to take on more distinct shape. It was a hypnotic sort of night. The intense cold put frost crystals on the barbed wire fences, on the fence posts. It made the air so clear and clean that everything seemed magnified. The stars looked like sparkling ice cubes. My breath was a plume of white, frosting whatever it touched. And I could feel my heart thumping solidly against my chest to send blood racing even to the ends of my fingers to keep them warm.

As I walked, I wondered if Molly would run, come down from the cave, and finding a coon trail, line out and bay to the moon about the excitement she felt. In a way, it was sad because the dog was surely a prisoner of her breeding and training. But then, I thought, aren't we all?

Perhaps she wouldn't run simply because there would be no raccoons abroad to pursue. In extremely cold weather, coons might sleep for days, or even weeks, living off accumulated fat and only peering out from their tree dens from time to time to see if the weather had moderated.

At the base of the first bluff, I slid out of the pack and my snowshoes to rest. Free of the fifty pounds, I felt light enough to fly to the top of the first bluff.

I found a snow-covered log, brushed a place

to sit, and looked up. Under the moonlight, the bluff seemed precipitous. The trees, leaning on their long shadows, seemed impenetrable. Of course, I knew it was an illusion—tricks which bright light and dark shadow can sometimes play. But just looking at it was enough to mesmerize the mind, make it forget reality and accept the fantasy, believe in what was only immediately obvious to the eye.

Rested, I got back into the pack straps and shrugged the load into place. I carried my snowshoes now, and began a slow, careful ascent. It was a painful climb. The unwieldy sack kept me off balance and, having but one hand free, I found it almost impossible to pull myself from tree to tree as I had during the day. Sometimes, I had to go to my knees and crawl, lest I slip backward, fall, and go bouncing back into a tree with what could be a rib-crushing crunch.

By the time I reached the summit, I was exhausted and wet with sweat. I lay in the snow to get my breath; then, I felt my strength come back. I also felt the cold air penetrate and chill my perspiration-soaked body.

If I lay there, I surely would freeze, so crawling to a tree, I pulled myself erect. I'd have to leave the snowshoes behind so I'd have both hands free to climb. I could pick them up on the way back.

Now I looked for tracks I'd made in the afternoon. I didn't want to get lost—not on such a cold night as this—so I walked west toward the river scrutinizing the ground.

I found my trail easily enough, and then I jammed my snowshoes into the snow so they were standing upright; I'd have no trouble locating them.

Following the tracks, I started to cross the bluff to begin my descent into the valley where Trout Creek flowed. At the edge, I stopped to survey the downward trail. It looked steeper than I remembered. I'd have to be careful, or, as my mother feared, I might fall, and then, who would find me?

Perhaps, if I backed down? That way I could hold to the brush—to the trees—and lower myself slowly. I was about to start when a movement in the valley made me hesitate.

Molly? I leaned forward. Perhaps a deer? A fox? Or had the shadows only played a trick on me?

I waited, but when there was nothing, I again got ready to make my descent. There it was again, and this time, I knew it was no trick of the moon, no shadow on the snow. This time I knew it for what it was—a man! A man following along the creek, walking the banks among the shadows down the valley slope.

12

My first impulse, upon discovering there was a man down in the valley of Trout Creek, was to rush down and accost him . . . Ask him what he was doing there. For an exciting moment, I had the feeling that he was trespassing on my domain, and I wanted not so much to ask him what he was doing, but how he dared to do it.

Then it occurred to me that he might feel that I was the trespasser—as I was—even though I didn't rightly know to whom the bluffs belonged.

After my first astonishment subsided, I stepped close to a tree so I might blend my body with its trunk. If he looked up, he would not see me. Standing there, I leaned forward and strained to get a better look and see if perhaps I might recognize him.

There was no chance of identification. His head was hidden by a high collar. He, too, was carrying snowshoes. Because of the way the moon played its shadowy tricks, I could not even guess at his size.

Still, my mind ran through the list of people whom I thought might have some reason for spooking around among the bluffs at night. There was George Reims, of course, or some of the men who had helped him run Molly out of Black Haw Woods. They could have heard her running coons, and realizing she was not dead, decided to come back and finish the job.

Nighttime would be ideal for such a hunt, especially if Molly were running a trail. Then with guns placed strategically, she might easily be ambushed.

Of course, it might be Matt Tabor. Perhaps he had heard the dog was running the bluffs with her litter of pups. Or, maybe Ted Feldman was interested in adding to his kennels. Hughie had seen him along the edge of Black Haw Woods, but that was no proof that he had been searching for the dog. He might have been training dogs of his own.

The only one I could eliminate was Bob

Bacon. He'd never have been able to make it across the snowy fields, much less climb the steep bluffs. Not even with a jug of wine to fuel his efforts.

Well, there was no point in speculating. Just thank goodness I hadn't rushed down and into view. For all I knew, it might even have been the sheriff or the conservation warden, especially if George Reims had reported that the sheepkiller was still alive.

Well, I couldn't go down in the valley now. The man might have companions, so I slipped out of the pack and braced it against a tree. I cleaned a place in the snow and sat down beside it. From where I sat, I could see the open creek winding darkly. If the cold hung on, it would eventually freeze, except in the swiftest runs.

After ten minutes, I had to get up to keep the cold from numbing me. I looked at my watch. One o'clock. Then I tramped a short path in the snow along the edge where I could keep watch, and began pacing to keep warm.

At one-thirty, when there had been no sign of any others, I decided it would be safe to proceed. I moved as quietly as possible—going from tree to tree—trying to stay in the shadows, pausing often to listen.

I made it to the valley floor without mishap, and after an interval of listening, started up the next slope. Once again, I was forced to crawl in some places; but now, with my hands free, I made better time.

It was two o'clock by the time I finally lowered myself into that fertile valley where Molly had been running. I was anxious now, and pressed on down the valley floor until I came to the clearly defined path which led up the sides of the next bluff to the cave.

I stood listening for awhile—and once a great horned owl hooted—and I couldn't stop the little shiver which rippled up my back even though the owl was a threat only to the rabbits and hares dining on woody stems among the brambles of the draws.

On my way up the bluff, I went slowly, pausing at intervals to whistle softly. Perhaps, I hoped that Molly would have had a change of heart and come down to greet me, the pups tumbling along behind.

All the way up, I watched for the dogs. When I could make out the dark entrance to the cave, I stopped climbing and waited. There was nothing. I climbed the rest of the way and, in front of the cave, scooped the snow away and spread the food.

Retreating a little way, I couldn't help but think what a relief it was to get rid of that fifty-pound load.

When I was what I considered a discreet distance from the cave, I took a position where I could watch. When no pups came out to the odor of feed, I surmised they weren't at home.

Perhaps Molly had taken them along when she went foraging for food. They were almost old enough now to accompany her on hunts, and if they had been the pups of a wolf, or coyote, or fox, they would be getting their first lessons in hunting.

Once again, the numbing cold was needling through my gloves, my boots. But here on the steep slope, there was no way of pacing to keep up my circulation.

Extreme cold can be deceptive. When a man is first exposed, he is exhilarated, made to feel doubly alive as his heartbeat increases. But when the first, fine feeling wears off, the laboring heart slows, and a not uncomfortable feeling of laziness pervades the body. It is the warning sign that unless a man gets up and moves, he is on his way to freezing to death.

In my cramped position on the steep bluff, huddled as I was against the bark of a shag hickory, I should have heeded those first warning signs, and moved at least as much as the terrain would permit.

But I didn't want to alarm the dogs if they came near, and furthermore, I was tired. Twice in the same day I had come through deep snow the long way to the bluffs, and twice in the same day, I had scaled the slopes.

Perhaps my resistance was lowered. Anyway,

when the first feeling of laziness made my legs and arms feel comfortably leaden, I welcomed it. The torpor was as delicious as a hot bath after a long, hard day. Huddled there, I didn't feel the cold, but only experienced a dreamy feeling of complete contentment.

Looking back now, I can remember that my mind, on several occasions, tried to rise above the dream world into which it was sinking. I suppose I even said to myself, "You've got to move or you're going to die."

But such is the stealth and cunning of death when it comes slyly on the silent wings of invisible cold. Defenses crumble, and instead of fighting with all his strength, a man actually welcomes the peace and quiet of the sleep which precedes the end.

Although I didn't know it then, the temperature had plummeted to thirty-five degrees below zero. Perhaps, if I hadn't been so tired, so completely worn out, I'd have been jarred into action by other warning signs around me.

I can remember several trees exploding from the cold, and the report of this cellular action must have been like cannon shots—though to my ears, they were only muffled thuds.

Then, too, ice bridged the last current in the busy little stream below me, cutting off its merry voice. I didn't notice.

If I'd only taken warning from the ice which

was building and building along one pants leg, because in my cramped position against the tree, my breath was laboring straight across one leg.

All I could think of was how utterly happy I was just to be curled up, there on the white slope. I didn't even think of watching for Molly. The trial I would soon have to face never crossed my mind. I was in a cocoon of contentment, and anyone who has not been there himself cannot possibly understand how utterly helpless I had become.

I remember closing my eyes from time to time and then abruptly opening them to stare at the moon which seemed so friendly—far up there beyond the bare branches—sailing smoothly in such a serene sky. I remember marveling over the way the frost had put an intricate webbing of white on a bush, how the shadows on the snow had finely scalloped edges.

My euphoria slipped into sleep, but who knows how long I slept? A minute? An hour? Two hours?

My arms were wrapped around my chest. My knees were pulled up to rest my head. Curled like a fetus, an unborn baby, I must have slipped farther, and farther, and farther away from the bluff above the valley, away from the world.

Molly's muzzle near my face was the first thing I saw when I next opened my eyes. Molly's muzzle and her long, white teeth and her blazing, black eyes. I could see she was barking by the puffs of white breath; then, I heard her as from a great distance.

I never did understand why she was barking. I expect one or another of the pups might have come around to the other side of the tree, and she thought I was trying to take them from her. Or perhaps, after all, she did know that I was dying, and being alarmed as animals sometimes are in the presence of death, she was making her protest.

All I know is that I was angry that she had bothered me, that she had broken the spell, lifted me from the deep, wonderful, carefree sleep. And I wanted her to go away, to leave me alone, to stop barking and showing her teeth.

Then when she wouldn't go, I tried to arouse myself enough to shout at her, to scare her away. I couldn't speak; all I could do was huddle there looking out through sleepy eyes so everything I saw was thinly veiled.

I tried to ignore her, go back to sleep, let her bark. But I couldn't do that either—so with as much exasperation as my lethargy would permit, I tried to strike out at her with my boots. It was a feeble effort. I could barely get my feet off the ground, much less kick in her direction. But it was enough to tip me off balance and to tilt me away from the trunk of the tree. When I started slipping, I couldn't even unfold my arms to save myself and went rolling like an unwieldy, awkward ball down the slope.

The first tree I hit straightened me out, but I was helpless to keep myself from slithering around and down the slope. I could not even bring my arms up over my face to protect it from the brambles which seemed to reach out and claw at it.

I doubt that I really felt those first jolts. I think my body was too numb. But, by then, I knew I was falling. My eyes were open, and the bluff, and the moon, and the trees were going around and around.

A rock outcropping jarred alive my first survival instincts. I must have taken the sharp pinnacle of rock right in the rib cage. I suppose it was like being slammed with a dull ax. Anyway, the pain got to me, swept the cobwebs from my mind, set my heart to racing so blood was once again rushing to my head, my arms, my legs.

Now I tried to save myself, but my body was beyond taking orders, and bushes and trees slipped from my grasp. I was fighting once again, fighting for that life which, only moments before, I had been willing to let go without lifting so much as a little finger to save it.

I must have been halfway down the long, steep bluff when my arms and legs began to respond; I felt coordination and strength returning to them. By then, too, I was beginning to be more conscious of pain.

Of course, pain has its purpose. It goads us into protecting ourselves, and now I wanted to put an end to the pummeling my body was taking. Now I wanted to stop the swift descent, stop it before I broke my head on a rock or my back against the trunk of a tree. So I dug in with my feet and hands, dug into the snow, the bushes, and the outcropping rocks. I slowed my downward progress, and though it seemed like forever, actually, it was only a matter of seconds before I came solidly up against the base of a tree and stopped.

Momentarily, I was stunned. The wind was knocked from my lungs, and I gasped for air. When I could breathe again, I looked down. The floor of the valley wasn't but fifty feet below. When I could think coherently, I wondered if any bones had been broken.

Using the tree to steady myself, I got up. My legs and arms worked. I was intact—alive and back from the threshold of death, apparently with nothing broken.

I couldn't trust myself to walk the rest of the way into the valley, so I sat and slid slowly, pushing myself from tree to tree and from rock to rock.

On the creek bank, I got up, kicked a hole in the thin ice of a rapids, stooped to splash icy water on my face. Then I knelt for a time, as though in prayer, before beginning the long, painful, almost impossible task of getting home . . .

13

The trip back was the most excruciating experience of my life. It was dawn when I came into the yard, and my father was leaving the house to get on with the chores. I started walking toward him; then, I felt my knees buckle. I saw the pinnacle of the house roof tilt slowly as if the structure were falling, and I fainted.

When I awakened, I was in my bed. Hot-water bottles were warm against my ribs and my thighs, and my mother was holding and rubbing my hands.

Standing over me were Dr. Albert Bussel

130

and my father. "Welcome back," the doctor said. I tried to smile, but the throb of pain through my body made me wince instead. "Who beat you up?" the doctor asked.

I shook my head. "Nobody," I managed to say.

"Then how come you're almost a solid mass of bruises?"

I looked up at my mother, thinking about how she had feared I'd fall off a cliff. "I slipped down a bluff. Fell almost to the bottom."

"Well, you look like you've been hit by a hundred hammers," the doctor said.

"I feel like it."

"Think you can eat?"

"I don't know."

"Can you make him some soup?" the doctor asked, turning to my mother.

She put my hands down gently and got up from the chair. "I've got some," she said. "I'll get it." She turned and left the bedroom.

"Molly saved my life," I said, looking straight at my dad. He only nodded. "I fell asleep and began to freeze to death. She went wild with barking and awakened me."

"Then you fell?" he asked. I nodded. "Well," he continued, "I've already called Mr. Benz. We're going to have to get a continuance. You can't appear in court tomorrow."

I said nothing. The doctor was taking my pulse. "I'm going to give you something for the pain and to make you sleep," he said, "but first you should eat. While we're waiting for the soup, do you mind telling me what you were doing up among the bluffs at night?"

I closed my eyes because it hurt to talk, so my dad told him.

"You're lucky to be alive," the doctor said. "It was thirty-five degrees below zero. It doesn't take long to freeze to death when it's that cold." My mother came in with the soup.

It was chicken-wing soup, rich and hot. She spooned it to my lips, and the heat of it seemed to loosen my muscles, but the pain continued to throb in waves from my toes to my head.

When I'd finished the soup, the doctor gave me an injection. "This will help," he said, turning to my father. "If he awakens he may be irrational, but don't let it worry you. It's powerful stuff. It sometimes makes the patient hallucinate or even do foolish things, but it eases the pain, and it provides him with the rest he needs, the rest he must have to heal."

Gradually, the pain receded; the room and the people in it became indistinct, fuzzy, and then I must have fallen asleep.

When I awakened, I knew it was late in the afternoon because the sun was so low it put a glow on a painting of ducks which hung high on the east wall of my bedroom. I was alone, and the house was unusually quiet—so quiet I could hear the clock downstairs in the living room ticking the time away.

My brothers should have been home from school, and I wondered why I didn't hear them. I raised to a sitting position and waited for the pain to subside; then, swinging my feet over to the side of the bed and putting them to the floor, I got up.

I wobbled for a moment, then got a grip on myself and started downstairs. It was almost time to do the chores, but nobody was home. I went into the kitchen and looked out a window. The machine shed door was open and the car was gone.

Going to the refrigerator, I took out the pitcher of milk and poured myself a glassful. It wasn't until I sat at the kitchen table to drink it that I saw the note:

"Danny. Now, you get right back to bed." My mother must have anticipated I'd be roaming around. There was more. "We've gone to town to get a postponement. Took the boys along so they wouldn't bother you. Now, get back to bed."

I had to laugh in spite of my aches and pains. It was typical of my mother to anticipate my actions. Getting up, I went into the bathroom and took two aspirin. Then I climbed the stairs back up to bed. It was a relief to sink back into the feathery mattress, to have it fold around me and feel the warmth creep down my legs to my feet.

The aspirin dulled the pain. I sat up and swung my legs out of bed. I had a strange, almost hypnotic feeling that, if I made the effort, I could solve the crime. Looking back, I suppose I was still feeling the effects of the shot the doctor gave me and the action of the aspirin.

At the time, however, I didn't realize that I was acting abnormally and that I should have stayed in bed. As I sat there, it occurred to me that, if I went back to the bluffs, I would find the murderer. If I got up, dressed, and went back out I might get there in time to catch the culprit.

Slowly, I got back into my clothes and, by the time I was dressed, I was limber enough to bend over and lace my boots without groaning.

My folks would be worried, perhaps even angry, but I had to take a chance. If the man who had been wandering through the bluffs came back, I wanted to be there. Perhaps then, I would know for certain who killed Jake Tabor.

When I was fully clothed, I went downstairs and sitting at the kitchen table wrote: "Dear Mom and Dad, I just have to find out who comes at night to roam the bluffs. I have a feeling that if I do find out, I will know who the killer is. I feel fine now. The more I move, the better I feel. So don't worry —please!"

I hurried into my sheepskin-lined jacket, my hunting cap, and my fleece-lined gloves. Taking my snowshoes down from the peg in the entryway, I went out into the yard just in time to see the sun slip down below the horizon.

Each mile, the walking became easier. My muscles seemed to loosen, and even the pain receded until what there was focused mostly in my head.

I got to the bluffs just as the moon changed from a dull bronze to a brilliant white, and leaving my snowshoes at the base of the first bluff, I started climbing.

The weather had moderated some. I guessed the temperature was probably holding steady at about zero, but I didn't feel the cold as I passed over the intricate pattern of shadows cast by the reaching, bare branches of the trees.

On top of the first bluff, I stood listening. There was nothing, nothing except some ice crystals which had lost their hold on a limb and were falling among the branches with a tinkling sound.

Still, I stood, scanning the next valley, listening—hoping to hear movement in the brush across the snow's crust. When there was nothing, I went down slowly into the next valley. Again, I waited, and when there was nothing, I started up the side of the next bluff.

It was when I was perhaps halfway up that I

thought I heard the crunch of snow off to the left. I dropped to my knees and, holding my breath, listened. There it was again—definite this time—someone walking—breaking through the snow's crust.

I went to my stomach and lay waiting. Then, from between two junipers, walked a big buck deer. His antlers had not yet been dropped and two plumes of white jetted from his nostrils—a magnificent animal looking to fill his stomach with the tiny, dormant buds which decorated the ends of all the bushes.

He came very near to me before catching my scent. Then he stood like a deer cast in bronze for several seconds before wheeling and racing away with an uncommonly quiet stride for such a huge animal.

I moved upward once more, as quietly as I could, from tree to tree. When I topped out, I crawled behind a windfall and lay listening. A horned owl sounded off so far away it came to me faintly like an echo. Then I thought I heard the whistle of a train many miles away, so faint it seemed the sound might only be in my head.

I was just about to get up and move over the top of the bluff to descend into the next valley, when something—I don't know what, because I heard nothing—made me stay where I was. I lay for what must have been five minutes, until I heard a branch crack—then I knew there was something out there among the trees.

I hunched down lower behind the windfall and waited. There it was—the brittle sound of crusted snow being broken. I raised my head a little, but I could see nothing. I crouched down again. Whatever—deer, man, or maybe only a little old fox—it was coming toward me.

Waiting until the sound was loud enough to exclude fox or even deer, I raised up again and, in silhouette, saw a man hunched over and moving slowly through the thick brush. From where I lay, I could see steam lifting from his collar—so he must have been sweating—and I could see his breath, white on the cold air. If he kept coming in a straight line, he would pass within a few feet of me.

I lifted my head higher, hoping for a good enough look to identify him. But his head was pulled low into his jacket collar, and the flaps on his cap kept the moonlight out of his face.

So I waited, and when he was within a few feet and I still hadn't recognized him, on impulse, I leaped and threw myself on his back, knocking him to the ground.

As he went down, I heard him grunt. Then I heard him say, "What the . . . !" Then we were wrestling.

It was no contest. My bruised and weakened body was no match for his. In seconds, he had me on my back and, sitting astride my middle, he pinned my arms to the ground.

His hat was askew; then, I recognized him. It was Ted Feldman! Ted Feldman! Field trial judge, hound dog man! Ted Feldman—almost twice as big as I was, and right now, just about the most angry man I'd ever met.

He must have recognized me at the same time I recognized him, because he said, "Why, you crazy kid. What's gotten into you? Are you insane?"

Then for maybe ten seconds we just stared at each other, the steam jetting from our mouths as we breathed hard from the exertion of the struggle. Then I felt his fingers relax on my arms. I felt his weight lift from my middle as he got up.

Erect, he stood over me, and I waited. Finally, he nudged me with a boot and said, "Get up!"

Slowly, I got to my feet. Then he asked, "Why'd you jump me?"

I was going to say, "Because you killed Jake Tabor, and because now you are trying to find his dogs." Instead, I said, "I thought you were someone else."

"Like whom, for instance?"

"Maybe Matt Tabor."

"And why would you want to jump Matt? Or anybody, for that matter?"

It was a good question, because why should I want to jump anyone? I hadn't really meant to jump Feldman. It just happened. There he was, going on by, and I didn't know who it was; so, I leaped out and pulled him down. I'll never know what impelled me to do it.

The moon was directly overhead now. The snow where we had rolled and wrestled was flattened and the shadows of the tree branches were not as distinct in that little area of combat as they were where the snow had not been disturbed.

Ted Feldman was adjusting his hat, pulling his collar back up. "So you know the dog is here, too," he finally said. When I didn't answer, he went on, "As a matter of fact, you've probably known where that dog and her pups have been all along, ever since the day you killed Jake."

"I didn't kill Jake!" I shot back at him, and with equal anger, "Maybe you did! Everybody knows you wanted that dog!" It all came out of me like a bullet from a gun, without thinking.

"You can't be serious. You can't believe I'd kill a man to get his dog!"

"Well, everyone knows you're crazy about dogs."

"Not crazy enough to kill Jake!"

"Then why do you come at night? Why not in daylight?"

"Because I have to work during the day. Because, you fool, I've got a grocery store and a feed store to take care of."

His sincerity turned my accusation aside so effectively that I felt foolish. "Well, maybe . . ." I said weakly. The effects of the medication must have worn off, because suddenly I wondered what I was doing out in the bluffs.

"You're crazy." Feldman said. Then after a short silence, he added, "Or maybe you're not so crazy after all. Maybe you figure if you can pin the murder on someone else, it will get you off the hook."

"You're dead wrong!" I was angry again. "I never killed Tabor, and I'm not looking to pin it on anyone except the guy who really did it."

"Well, you're looking at the wrong man. I may want Tabor's dog. In fact, Matt said if I found him, he'd sell him to me. But killing? You crazy kid, you'd better watch what you're saying."

What could I say? I had to say something. Before I could think of anything, Feldman said, "You know, at first, I couldn't believe you really killed Tabor. But now I'm not so sure." With that, he abruptly turned his back on me and started to walk back in the direction from which he had come. All I could do was stand there feeling like a fool and watch him go. When I could no longer hear his boots crunching the snow crust, I turned and started back myself.

140

It was near morning—although still dark—when I got back. The house was ablaze with lights, and although I was apprehensive at how my folks would react to my foolhardy venture, I was glad to get back. All the pain was there again, sweeping up my calf muscles into my thighs, through my belly and my back to come thumping into my head.

14

I stayed in bed for two days. The bruises turned from black to a sickly yellow. Every time I got up to go to the bathroom, my mother would come hurrying to see that I got back into bed.

At first, when I walked in that early morning after my confrontation with Feldman, I thought my father was going to add to the bruises already on my body—he was that angry.

"What were you thinking? What was wrong with your head!" he shouted. "You must have still been dopey from the shot Doc gave you to do a thing like that. You could easily have died out there."

Perhaps I could have, but finally, the specter of spending years in prison was becoming a very personal, frightening prospect; at last, I could feel that it was actually happening to me and that I wasn't just an actor playing an utterly ridiculous part in a melodramatic play.

I HAD BEEN ARRESTED FOR MURDER. I HAD HAD A PRELIMINARY HEARING AND BEEN BOUND OVER FOR TRIAL. I WAS TO BE TRIED. THE EVIDENCE ALL POINTED TO MY GUILT. I HAD NO DEFENSE WORTH MENTIONING. AND SO, I, A SEVENTEEN-YEAR-OLD BOY, MIGHT BE PUT IN PRISON FOR FIVE OR TEN YEARS, OR EVEN FOR THE REST OF MY LIFE.

It would mean never coming to the edge of a meadow, sparkling with dew, to watch the cows come lazily up out of the lush, grassy bottoms. It would mean never sitting in the dark quiet of the barn with a cat pressing against the calf of my leg as I became sleepy from the animal warmth around me.

There would be no crisp fall mornings in my duck blind in a slough of the Bloodstone River waiting for the circling mallards; seeing the blue-bills come hurtling in among my decoys on stubby wings; watching Panther launch himself with a tremendous splash to retrieve a duck which had come tumbling out of the sky.

There would be no quiet evenings in the living room in front of the television set being carried away by a movie to some exotic world while I munched on popcorn; listening to my mother making her knitting needles click and my father puffing reflectively on his pipe.

Life as I knew it would end. There would be a bare cell with a bench bed and a naked toilet bowl. There would be the low murmur of a hundred, a thousand, other men talking in undertones in a hundred, a thousand, cells. There would be a number on my back, and I was old enough to know that if I stayed in prison long enough, the number would be carved right into my heart; I would no longer be Danny Stuart but a grim ghost of my old self, aging without hope or love.

It had come to me, I think, while I lay on the side of the steep bluff freezing. It had finally seeped through my natural, youthful optimism while my mind was off-guard, slipping into that lethargy which precedes death.

The specter had remained—and I saw my parents turning white and becoming bent, and finally, lying down to die, sorry almost that they had ever lived, because, with me in prison, a part of them and their world would cease to be.

Maybe that's why I hadn't been able to lie in bed and await the inevitable. Perhaps that's why I had risen above my pains to go back out onto the high bluffs, hoping—foolishly perhaps—that there, when the moon was high, out there among the crooked shadows, I would find the answer to my dilemma, the key to my freedom.

144

So what now? Lying there with the shadows starting to creep out of the corners of my bedroom, I couldn't see even a pinprick of hope in the wall of gloom which had closed around me. As Mr. Benz had said, "The best we can hope for is that the judge will be lenient. Perhaps he will take your age into consideration and believe that you have always been a good boy. Maybe he will understand that you are no threat to society and give you a light sentence—maybe five, not more than ten years."

Ten years! I'd be twenty-seven. To me that was old, old, old. By twenty-seven, a man could have a family of three, or four, or five children. He could have his own farm, his own herd of Guernseys, his own chicken flock, sheep, pigs, ducks . . .

My mother came into the bedroom. She had Panther with her. "He's so lonesome all he does is sit by the door. He won't even eat."

When the dog saw me, he was on the bed in a single leap. He kissed me with his tongue, pawed at me, and his thick tail swung a wild arc that sent a bedside lamp from its table to the floor.

My mother tried to pull him off, but he was too big for her. I wound my arms around his neck and pulled him down on my chest.

"Easy now. Easy now. Hold it, Panther. Hold it."

Gradually, he quieted and lay beside me, his eyes sparkling and his long tongue hanging from the side of his muzzle, dripping beads of excitement to the quilt.

"Well, you sure cured him quick," my mother said after the dog had quieted down.

I laughed and answered, "I think he cured me, too." The gloom had been dispelled from my mind, because here was life, love, devotion; I thought to myself that maybe I could even take these things to prison with me if I learned how to protect and cherish them in my mind.

"Well, he can't stay here," my mother said. She had a thing about dogs in the house.

But a voice from the doorway behind her said, "Not even for a little while?" It was my father, and even he was smiling; the taut look had gone from his face, and a little color had come back to his cheeks.

"Well, maybe for a little while," my mother said, smiling. "But on the rug beside the bed. It isn't healthy for a dog to be in someone's bed."

I don't know where she got that notion. Perhaps from her mother. I edged Panther off the bed, he thumped down on the rug, and I dangled a hand over the side to scratch his ears.

Dad came and got the dog after supper. After a run, he brought him back to me. He smelled fresh, like the snow and the wind.

"Tomorrow I'm getting up," I announced.

"Sure you're strong enough?"

"Positive."

"Well, okay. But no trip to the bluffs."

"Molly's got fifty pounds of food. It'll last a week. I can wait a couple more days."

"Perhaps Feldman has found her."

"He won't catch her now. And, anyway, if he had, we'd have heard," I said.

"I suppose so."

Panther grunted, put his head down on his forepaws, and fell asleep. I reached over to turn off the light; then, in the dark, I resolved that no matter what happened, I wouldn't quit hoping. I would live for each day with the thought that there were better ones to come. After that, I had the most peaceful, uninterrupted sleep I'd had since Sheriff Dobbie Stotz first came to the place and announced he had a warrant for my arrest!

The good feeling I had taken to sleep with me was still there in the morning; so, instead of waiting for my mother to bring breakfast, I got into my clothes.

Panther, on seeing me get dressed, was beside himself with joy. I suppose he figured we might be taking a walk into Black Haw Woods or down to the Bloodstone River.

I should have, of course, had traps along the river. Every fall and winter I trapped mink, muskrats, weasels, and, sometimes, I took a beaver or two from the little colony near the source of Dead Creek. In five years of trapping, I had made more than two thousand dollars. It was to have been used for my tuition to the University of Wisconsin College of Agriculture, but now I intended it to help my parents pay Mr. Benz for my defense.

I supposed I could still take a hike along the river. It might help keep my mind off the trial. There would be no point, however, in setting traps. The trial was three days away, and who'd tend them when I had to be in court—and afterward?

My mother was surprised to see me down for breakfast, and when my dad came up from the barn after doing chores, he asked, "Think you're up to it?"

"I feel good," I said. "Lying in bed just makes me weaker. Maybe I'll walk on down to the river and scout around. Sort of map out a trapline so I can get busy when the trial's over."

No one said a word. We all just stood there looking as the impact of my hopeless situation held us apart. My mother broke the tension by dropping a spoon. Then my father became effusive, "That's right," he said, "you go down there. You look for sign. You map out a trapline. When the trial is over, you can get your traps set. You can skip chores mornings before school and evenings so you can run the line. You go down to the river so you'll be ready. Take your time. Take a sandwich. Take

148

Panther . . ." His voice trailed off, and there were no more words. What had been said hung between us even heavier than the silence because we all knew that there probably would be nothing after the trial—nothing but prison.

It was my mother again who came to the rescue. "Well, we've got to eat," she said, scraping the legs of a chair across the floor and sitting down. "If you're going down to the river, you've got to eat."

15 The Arctic front which had brought the biting cold had shattered up against southern winds, and as Panther and I started out of the yard, a little water was dripping from the eaves of our long, red barn. The snow underfoot was too soft for snowshoes so we went slowly, following game trails when possible. It was an easy, comfortable walk to the river.

On the way, we heard blue jays celebrating the reprieve from winter's cold, and there were chickadees in the spruce and nuthatches rattling the dry weed stalks. We saw two deer in their winter coats of drab gray, and it occurred to me that we hadn't even shot a buck for the freezer as had been our custom for as long as I could remember.

At the far edge of Black Haw Woods, I climbed a little rise so I could look down on the river. Screwtail Rapids had opened up again and was a thrust of black water in the otherwise white apron of snow that covered the ice.

Some buffleheads—we called them butterballs—and a small flock of goldeneyes—we called them whistlers—were diving for mollusks in the open water. I knew they'd stay for the winter, retreating during cold snaps only so far south as the river rapids, which hadn't frozen, and hurrying back when the weather moderated.

Somebody was fishing through the ice just off Deer Track Peninsula right in the first sweep where the river formed the oxbow. I supposed it was Hughie Frazer. From where I stood, he was little more than a dark spot against the snow, moving sometimes as he went from hole to hole to inspect his tip-ups.

Coming down off the knoll into the marsh, I moved from muskrat house to muskrat house, determining which had occupants by scraping snow from the ice to look for their bubble trails.

Several houses had been invaded by muskrat-hungry mink, and paw prints of the little killers were in the snow. In several places, muskrats had come out from beneath the ice to leave tail-dragging trails to where they went below again.

There was one set of raccoon tracks; it reminded me of Molly and the realization that soon I'd have to be hauling food back in to her.

Without consciously meaning to, I was gradually closing in on Hughie. Perhaps it was curiosity now that I knew he had once been sweet on my mother; or perhaps, it was the need to talk to someone other than my parents and my two small brothers.

Hughie sat on a tiny, canvas camp stool wearing a huge bearskin coat, moth-eaten and with bare patches of hide showing at the elbows and where the cavernous pockets began. He had a windbreak of canvas stretched between two poles, but it stood off to one side because the sun was shining and the day was warm.

"What happened to you?" Hughie asked, noting the bruises on my face.

"Slipped off a bluff."

"Looking for that hound dog, I suppose?"

"That's right."

"Find her?"

I nodded.

"Pups with her?"

I nodded again.

"Gone wild, eh?"

152

"Yes, she's gone wild."

A red tip-up flag snapped upright and fluttered in the southern wind. Hughie got up from his camp stool and walked over to the hole in the ice. He took the fishline between a forefinger and thumb, lifted tentatively, and then, after a sharp jerk, pulled a perch out onto the ice. It flopped about, its yellow sides and orange fins bright in the sun. He carefully unhooked the fish, took pliers from the depths of one of his coat pockets, and killed the fish by striking it on the head. He then tossed it in a small galvanized pail where a half dozen other fish were yellow, and black, and orange.

He rebaited the hook with a tiny, white grub, let it slither through the hole into the black water, put the tip-up flag down, and set the spring so it would release the flag if a fish pulled on the line. He sat back on his camp stool.

"Trial is day after tomorrow?" Hughie made it a question.

"Yeah, day after tomorrow."

"You scared?"

"You bet I am."

Hughie looked off over the ice, across Deer Track Peninsula to where Black Haw Woods stood black in its winter nakedness.

"They'll never convict you," Hughie said. The pronouncement startled me. Everyone else assumed I would be convicted, and here was Hughie Frazer announcing that I would be found not guilty.

I didn't want to talk about the trial, so I didn't press him for such reasons as he might have been harboring concerning the outcome. Instead, I called Panther back, as he had wandered far down the frozen river on the trail of something or other.

But Hughie wouldn't let it alone. "Just believe me," he said, "when I tell you they won't convict you."

Another red flag snapped upright signaling a bite, but I didn't follow along to watch him lift the perch out this time. My mind was back on the trial. A cloud slid across the face of the sun, and I shivered in its shadow.

Well, Hughie was wrong, of course. His belief only gave credence to the talk that, over the years, he had been gradually substituting his own dreams for reality; that he had, as some said, started becoming a little soft in the head.

I didn't quite believe that, but I could understand how a man like Hughie, living alone as he did, might come to view the world in soft shades of complacency. What could bother a man whose most important job was to catch a few fish?

When Hughie came back with the perch, I remembered to relay my mother's thanks for the walleyed pike he had sent along the last time we'd met.

154

His head came up out of his great bearskin coat and the deep lines in his face took a softer slant as he smiled shyly. "Did she like them?" he asked.

"Yes, she did," I said, "and she says that any time you drop by, there'll be a pie or a cake for you to take along."

He went to the windbreak then and took the perch from a bucket and put them into a bag. "For her," he said, handing them to me.

I thanked him for the fish, whistled for Panther, and then started back off the ice toward the marsh and Deer Track Peninsula.

Even while I walked, the warm southerly wind put a haze over the sun, and the frozen marsh was once again a dreary place. When I was back on the rise, I turned. Hughie was hunched like a great bear on the tiny camp stool, watching for a red flag to signal that yet another perch had accepted the tiny, white grub—offerings I knew Hughie collected himself from out of the hearts of milkweed pods.

I couldn't help wondering, as I walked, how Hughie had come to such a narrow trail in life, a trail which led from his one-room shack to the river and back again without intersections, or side trails, or any hills or valleys—a single, solitary, straight path. I wondered if it had been because of my mother. That path made him a prisoner just as surely as anyone who had been jailed. I wondered if

155

he had chosen the solitary, uneventful life because he still loved my mother. And if that were true, I wondered if my mother knew about it.

It wasn't yet noon when I came to the edge of Black Haw Woods, and I wondered if I should make a quick trip into the bluffs to see how Molly and her pups were doing. The walk to the river had eased the soreness out of my legs; the only remnants of pain were in my back muscles, which wasn't enough to impede my progress.

My parents surely would not approve, but it seemed to me that I was old enough to make some decisions without consulting them. If I cut cross-country now, I would be home before dark, and unless they asked me, I just wouldn't say anything about it.

I looked to the sky for weather signs. There were no snow clouds, only a thin haze—transparent as an onion skin—pulled across the sun.

So I turned north where a deer trail followed a fence line. The whitetails had trampled the snow well enough so it was easy walking. In the distance, I could see the bluffs, their tops indistinct in the haze, and now I bent forward, swinging into that ground-consuming stride I had mastered while running my traplines before and after school.

Panther soon tired of making side trips to examine errant odors in the snow and fell in behind me since the going was easier. We came to the foot of the first bluff within an hour, and although I was perspiring and breathing hard, I didn't rest but went right up.

Careful not to fall, I moved swiftly into the first draw through which Trout Creek flowed. The warm weather had opened sections of it, and the water made small musical sounds as it curled around rocks and up against the ice-bound shores.

I paused in the valley to catch my breath then started up the other side. It was steep, and thawing snow made it treacherous. I moved slowly, making certain to have a tree or bush to grab onto in case I started sliding.

By the time I reached the top, I knew I was not in as good physical condition as I had surmised. I was breathing hard and the muscles in my calves and thighs seemed leaden. I had come this far so there was no reason now to turn back.

It was easier going down into the valley where Boiling Water Creek was making angry little sounds about the obstructions in its path. When I got to the bottom, I drank from the stream which had broken out of its vise of ice for as far as I could see.

After resting, I started slowly downstream, watching for signs. There were dog tracks everywhere—Molly's and those of her five pups.

When I came to where they had beaten a

trail up the side of the next bluff to their cave, I sat down to listen. Panther, already having scented the dogs, started up the bluff, and I had to call him back. He sat beside me then, bright-eyed and anxious, his thick tail beating out a fan-shaped imprint in the snow.

High above, I heard a hawk keening. It had probably returned on the southerly wind to the valley because it was a hunting paradise for the big predator birds. Crows were bickering somewhere down near where I knew the Bloodstone River flowed, and nearby, I heard a ruffed grouse ticking off sharp little clucks with the precision of a clock.

Panther left me again to start up the trail, so I followed. The higher we got, the faster my black dog's tail wagged. When we were almost to the cave, Panther whined, and I thought I heard an answering whine from somewhere in the brush.

When I came into the tiny clearing where I could see the cave mouth, there was nothing except a small mound of dog food which Molly and her family hadn't eaten yet.

Panther went straight to the mouth of the cave, stuck his head in, and whined. A growl backed him up, and he retreated a few feet before sitting to cock his head and tilt his ears as if perplexed. Then he whined again, and his query was answered.

I waited, half lying, half sitting on the side of the steep bluff thinking to let Panther make all the overtures since neither Molly nor her pups would have anything to do with me.

When Molly didn't show at the cave entrance, Panther went forward again and put his head into the opening. Once more, he was warned away with a growl. This time, when he retreated, he lay down as though to wait out the hound—to let her make the next move.

It wasn't Molly who came to the cave entrance first but her pack of pups all crowding one another for a look at Panther.

The black dog lifted his head and whined an invitation. All five pups whined impatiently, and then, as if on some prearranged signal, they charged out and, in an ecstasy of reunion, smothered Panther with puppy paws and puppy tongues.

Panther stood so as to be above their enthusiasm, his tail up and out of the way but wagging happily, his head held high so the pups could not get at his ears.

While the pups were pinwheeling around the black dog, Molly appeared at the cave entrance. Panther gave her a short, anxious bark; again, she answered with a growl.

The growl stopped the pups in their tracks, and they all turned to look at their mother. Four of them started toward her, but the biggest male stood his ground, and when he again began assaulting Panther with mock wrath, the four turned their backs on Molly and joined him.

159

Perhaps chagrined, Molly's tail came tighter between her hind legs, but then she ran nervously from the cut in the rocks. Halfway to the black dog, she stopped. Panther whined encouragement. She took another several steps, and her tail came out from between her legs and wagged tentatively.

Panther yipped with obvious joy and walked up to her. She cringed, but when he put his nose to her muzzle, she stood upright, and then suddenly all seven dogs were whirling about on the steep side of the bluff in an unrestrained celebration!

It was my time to creep closer without being noticed, and I did. Then when they paused for breath—all their long, pink tongues lolling—I was among them. When they began playing again, the pups fell over my legs, plumped into my lap, and I had to hang onto a tree lest they send me tumbling down the side of the bluff.

The next time they paused for breath, Molly's head wasn't inches from mine, so I said, "Good dog, Molly. Good dog." She looked at me as though seeing me for the first time. When her tail started to come down to be tucked between her legs, I repeated, "Good dog, Molly. Good dog."

She didn't tuck her tail away but wagged it slowly a few times, and then looked as if to see if I'd noticed. "Good dog, Molly," I said, and then when I felt her tongue on my cheek, I knew that in one little area of my troubled world, I had won a

160

victory. Molly would come in with me, and so would her pups, anytime I was ready to bring them in.

16 The cold returned on Wednesday, the day before the trial. It came during the night on a shift of wind. I hardly noticed as most of my day was spent in Mr. Benz's overheated office as he explained to me how I was to conduct myself during the trial.

I thought his instructions were ridiculous. I didn't want to sit there looking like the picture of injured innocence. I couldn't, in the first place. All I wanted was to tell my side of the story exactly as it had happened—no dramatics—just the straightforward truth, and I told him as much.

"But I already told you, nobody's going to

believe your story," he said. "In the face of the evidence they've got against you, nothing short of a miracle is going to save you unless you can get the jury to sympathize with you, feel that you, even if guilty, are really nothing but a sad, naïve, somewhat stupid boy who really only needs guidance and certainly not punishment."

It was the word "stupid" that made me lose my temper. At any rate, I lit into Mr. Benz and told him I wasn't going to pass myself off as an ignorant clod, that I was aware of the charges and of the serious consequences which a guilty verdict might bring.

It was then my father cut in. "Can't we dispense with a jury trial?" he asked. "Can't we waive our rights to a jury, and just have the judge sit in judgment?"

Mr. Benz threw up his hands. "A judge," he said, "would rule strictly on the legal aspects of the case. The law would be all that counts with him. Our only chance is with a jury, and our only hope is that we can get enough women on that jury who are soft and sympathetic enough to plead your case with the other jurors. If we can get enough women on the jury, maybe, we can play on their emotions, get at their motherly instincts, get them mad enough at Jake Tabor, who, after all, was really a brute—get them mad enough to believe he deserved even killing."

Dad said, "That's dishonest. That's worse

163

than telling a lie. That's like trying a dead man when he can't even be there to protest, to protect himself!"

It made me sick. This wasn't a trial to come by a just verdict. This was a fight. My lawyer and, therefore, I were going to stoop to all kinds of cheap tricks to get me my freedom instead of telling the plain, unvarnished truth and then letting the jurors decide who was lying.

Attorney Benz suddenly became quite calm. "Let me tell you," he began in a quiet voice, "you are fighting for your right to live a normal life. You are a cornered animal. You have every right in the world to use every tactic available to you to guarantee the right to live like a human being. The district attorney is going to do everything within his power to show you as an irresponsible, good-for-nothing delinquent who would kill any man for revenge. If you think the truth is going to help you in that courtroom tomorrow, you're crazy, because no one is going to believe what you call the truth." My father put up his hand as though to stop him, but Mr. Benz began talking faster and louder.

"When you sit on trial, two men are going to swear that you threatened to kill Jake Tabor. Sheriff's witnesses are going to testify that they found your knife with Tabor's blood on it, and that, by your own admission, it was your knife. They're going to testify they found your boot tracks at the scene of the crime, and in fact, that you admitted to being in a field right next to the woods in which Jake was killed—and at the time he was killed . . . And then they're going to have some surprises for you," Mr. Benz continued. "Surprises I can't even begin to guess at, but which likely will put some shadow of doubt on your past behavior. They may come up with little incidents which you have long forgotten, showing that you weren't always polite to your teachers; that you did sometimes quarrel, and even fight, with your classmates; that you have a violent temper; that you are an impulsive person doing things on the spur of the moment without considering the consequences . . ."

Mr. Benz paused to get his breath. He had been talking in sharp, staccato bursts, but now there wasn't a sound in the office except the ticking of a tiny desk clock. Out of the corner of my eye, I could see my mother dabbing at tears on her cheeks with a small handkerchief. I could see the rigid line of muscle along my dad's jaw and the line of white around his lips.

Finally, Mr. Benz spoke again; but this time, his voice was subdued, his words spaced. "I know it isn't a pretty picture. But that's the way it is—that's what we've got to be prepared for. That's what we've got to fight against."

Once again, the office was quiet. I expected

165

my father to say something, but he didn't. Again, it was up to the attorney to break the silence. He rang for his secretary and when she came in, he said, "Get coffee."

She backed out, and my mother who had been holding back, finally sobbed. My father fumbled in his pocket for his pipe, and I leaned back, tired and beaten as if I'd just fallen down the bluff again—bouncing from rock to rock, tree to tree, being torn by prickly ash, scratched by briars.

Within minutes, Mr. Benz's secretary was back with coffee in paper cups. It was scalding, and though it seared my lips, I drank some anyway. A sharp pain ran all the way down to my stomach.

Then we got on—in what seemed like a cold, calculating businesslike way—with lining up the witnesses who would appear in my behalf. Mostly, they were character witnesses: Professor Deane Proffer, principal of the high school; several teachers who had had me in their classes over the years; Reverend Jerome Weems, pastor of our church; and then, there was the proprietor of the hardware store who would testify that over the years he had sold hundreds of knives like the one which killed Jake Tabor; and a laboratory technician who would testify that my knife did not have human blood on it and that it had been lying in the grass for a long time.

There were a few others, but I was, in fact, going to be the principal witness in my own defense. "Now," Mr. Benz said, "when you are on the stand, it is your chance to tell the truth. When I question you, you will tell exactly how you lost and found your knife, exactly what you said after Jake grabbed you in the barn and after he kicked your dog, exactly what you were doing the day he was killed . . . everything, the whole truth, straight and factual. I'll take care of softening up the jury, of getting the women on our side when I question the character witnesses, and in my summation. Do you think you can do it?"

I nodded.

"Think you can stick to your story if the district attorney starts ripping into you, implying that you are a liar, that you'd say just about anything to save your hide? Think you can do it?"

Suddenly, I wasn't so sure. "I don't know," I said.

"Well, whatever you do, don't lose your temper. You've got one, you know. And it would serve the D.A.'s purpose to see you lose it. That's exactly what he would like you to do. If he cross-examines you, he may try every trick in the books to get you mad, to get you to flare up, to lose control, so he can point to you and say to the jury that you are a hothead likely to do anything—murder even—if pressed hard enough." He paused, and then asked, "Do you understand? Do you know what I'm trying to tell you?"

"I know," I said, "I know."

It was nearly five o'clock and dark by the time we got out of the attorney's office. I never realized how profusely I had been sweating until the harsh winds of evening hit me as we came out onto the street, and I shivered.

All the way home, there was just the sound of the car, the rattle of a loose door, and metallic complaints from the glove compartment—no one spoke.

That night was a dismal one. Mother put my two brothers to bed early, and we sat in front of the television watching an old movie, *The Hunchback of Notre Dame*, but I doubt that any of us really knew what the movie was about. Our thoughts were on the trial, on what tomorrow would bring, and then the day after, and the day after that . . . stretching, it seemed, into a gray, gray eternity of time.

Later, in bed, I couldn't get warm. I curled into a ball and put my hands to my feet, but my hands were cold, too. Finally, I got up, and without a light, felt my way downstairs, through the dining room into the kitchen. I was all the way into the kitchen before I realized my parents were there, too, sitting at the kitchen table in the dark.

"So you couldn't sleep either," my father said.

My mother got up and turned on a little night-light above the stove. It shone like a small star against the blue kitchen wall, and we all three cast huge shadows against the drawn window shades.

"I'll warm some milk," my mother said. She got up, rattled pans, opened the refrigerator and the little light flashed forth like lightning. I heard the milk gurgle from the pitcher; then, I saw the dull, red glow of the electric stove getting brighter and brighter beneath the shining saucepan.

Mother set three glasses on the kitchen table, and using a dish towel to keep from burning herself, she took the pan from the stove and poured the milk. The bright stove burner slowly lost color until I could no longer see it.

"Drink," my father said. "Maybe it will help."

"Wait," my mother said, "I'll get aspirin for each of us. Maybe they'll help us sleep."

I washed the aspirin down with a swallow of milk.

"This is stupid," my father finally said, "wasting our energy like this. The trial may last a long time. We'll need all the strength we've got."

Panther must have heard my father's voice, because he whined from his place in the entryway, and then he scratched at the kitchen door.

"He knows something is wrong," I said.

"Of course, he knows," my father agreed.

Cold crept along the kitchen floor from beneath the door. I curled my feet, one over the other, to get them warm. Then I said, "I just can't get warm. I've been cold all night."

My mother got up and went to the bathroom. When she came back she had one of the red hot-water bottles. She went to the kitchen sink, let the water run until it was steaming and filled the water bottle. She wrapped a dishcloth around it and handed it to me. "Here," she said, "take this to bed with you. Maybe it will help."

I didn't know. Even the warm milk in my stomach seemed to do no good. It just seemed to lie there like a lump of something solid.

My dad got up. "Let's try to sleep . . . We've got to get some sleep."

We all went back to our rooms, and I crawled beneath the quilts, sank into the feather ticking, and holding the hot-water bottle close to my stomach, curled so I was almost wrapped around it.

Just before I fell asleep, I thought I heard a dog from a long, long way off. It came on that winter night into my bedroom until an airplane flew over low and drowned out the sound.

Or maybe I didn't hear a dog at all. Maybe the wailing was in my mind—sad and forlorn, marked as I was by some perverse twist of fate to stand tomorrow before the people of Coulee City as the murderer of Jake Tabor.

That first morning in the courtroom, I know I was surprised to see that District Attorney Mark Fessler didn't look like an ogre, but seemed a **17**

kindly man. He was tall and straight with graying hair and huge hands which swept through the air as though to give impetus to his words.

Judge Hallock was equally human—bald, with a white fringe of hair and weather-reddened features, he leaned forward in his black robe to listen intently to everything that was said.

Most surprising was the dignity with which Mr. Benz conducted himself. During the week before the trial, I had first thought of him as being weak and ineffectual. Then I had seen him as a ruthless man who would stoop to any chicanery to win his case. But now he was patient, soft-spoken, questing, it seemed, for the truth from each juror as he questioned them adroitly and politely.

The district attorney was equally patient and polite. He made no objections to any of the prospective jurors being questioned. Mr. Benz challenged several men and, by this maneuver, was able to have his jury of twelve include four women.

When they were seated in the jury box and the trial was about to begin, I took my first good look at them, thinking, "Well, in their hands rests my fate. They can set me free, let me go back to the farm, and Panther, and the forest, and Molly. They can let me go out in the darkness every morning to go as far as the river by the first light in time to check my traps, or they can put me away in a gray place of no stars nor any morning with a sunrise.

It was hard for me to understand how twelve people could have so much power. Sitting there beside Mr. Benz in front of the long, shiny table, I thought they looked like all the ordinary people I had always known—people like the butcher, the car dealer, the bank clerk, the woman who lived on the farm next door. I even knew some of them by sight. They were people I'd passed often, I supposed, in the streets, or even sat next to

172

in a theater. Except that now they weren't neighbors but a tribunal sitting in judgment, a panel of people which by its vote could lock me away for life.

The selection of the jurors went swiftly. It was over by noon. The court recessed and Mr. Benz took my mother, father, and me to the Seashell Inn for lunch. It was a place of quiet men in conservative business suits, a place of women with carefully combed hair, a place of waitresses who came quietly on the thickly carpeted floor and spoke almost in a whisper.

Mr. Benz ordered a shrimp dish for all of us. I took one bite but couldn't eat anymore, so I asked for a glass of milk. I noticed my mother and father only picked at their food but that Mr. Benz was eating heartily.

Court resumed at one-thirty, and the district attorney began putting witnesses on the stand. It was precisely as Mr. Benz had predicted. The sheriff's deputies told how they'd first found the body. A coroner said death was the result of stab wounds, probably with a knife. A laboratory technician testified blood on the knife was human blood and of the same type as that of the dead man's. A sheriff's sergeant testified that I had admitted ownership of the knife which was found near the body. It went on, right down the line, exactly the way Mr. Benz had predicted it would happen.

Matt Tabor came to the stand and told

about the altercation I'd had with his father in the barn, and how I'd said, ". . . someday I'm going to kill you. . . ."

Then there was a break in the mass of evidence piling up against me. Bob Bacon came to the stand, and he appeared confused. When questioned by the district attorney, he said he *thought* I had said I would kill Jake Tabor. The district attorney, perhaps sensing he had a weak witness, quickly ended the questioning.

But Mr. Benz saw his chance and, during the cross-examination, he really tore into Bacon:

"You say you *thought* you heard the defendant say he would kill Jake Tabor." He emphasized the word "thought."

"Well, I guess I did," Bacon said.

"You *guess* you did." He emphasized the word "guess."

"Well, I wasn't that close."

"Then maybe you didn't hear anything?"

"Well, I heard something."

Mr. Benz took a new tack. "Who told you to say Danny Stuart threatened to kill Jake Tabor?"

Bacon looked wildly about. He pushed at the fringe of hair which came down over his forehead. He began sweating. "Your Honor," Mr. Benz addressed the judge, "I request this witness be instructed to answer the question."

The judge turned. "Mr. Bacon, you will answer the question."

"What was the question?" Bacon asked.

The judge turned to the court reporter. "Please read the question." The court reporter looked at the testimony and then read, "Who told you to say Danny Stuart threatened to kill Jake Tabor?"

Bacon was silent. "Well?" the judge intoned.

"Nobody told me," Bacon finally said. Then he looked down at the floor and refused to lift his eyes when Mr. Benz asked:

"Where were you standing when you heard Danny Stuart speak?"

"In the barn."

"Where in the barn in relation to the defendant?"

"I don't know."

"Well, were you close to him or far away?"

"I can't remember."

"Isn't it a fact," Mr. Benz said cuttingly, pointing a finger, "that Danny Stuart said, 'Someday *somebody* is going to kill you'? Isn't that a fact —that he said '*somebody*'?"

"Well, maybe. It's hard to remember. It's been a long time."

"Do you drink much?" Mr. Benz asked.

"Objection!" the district attorney shouted.

"Your Honor," Mr. Benz explained, "it is my purpose to show that this man was a virtual slave to the Tabors because they kept him supplied with alcohol."

"Objection overruled."

"I repeat the question," Mr. Benz said. "Do you drink much?"

Bacon nodded.

"Speak up," Mr. Benz said.

"Yes, I suppose I do," Bacon said, falteringly.

"Are you employed?"

"Sometimes."

"By whom?"

"The Tabors."

"Do they pay you in cash?"

"Sometimes."

"Well, when they don't pay you in cash, what do they pay you with?"

Bacon looked up at the judge as if for help. Then he looked at the district attorney. The judge said, "You'll have to answer."

"Mostly wine," Bacon said.

"You can't live without wine. You had wine before you came in here today. If you went a day without wine, you'd collapse. You wouldn't be able to function. Is that right, Mr. Bacon?"

Bacon had his head in his hands. The district attorney was on his feet, objecting.

"No more questions."

A bailiff helped Bacon from the stand to his seat. Within minutes, he got up and shuffled silently out.

Court was adjourned then, and Mr. Benz walked with us out into the corridor. "Try to get some sleep tonight," he said. "Tomorrow may be a rough day."

The next day was a rough day, and I had slept little. Most of the night, I had just lain there, trying to tell myself that all this couldn't be happening; that I, Danny Stuart, was having a terrible nightmare and that I would eventually wake up.

It wasn't a nightmare, and the next day the courtroom was crowded to overflowing. What little ground we might have seemed to have gained by Bob Bacon's indecision was soon lost when Charles Combs was called to testify that he once had a furious fight with me.

It was true. We had fought, and when I had seen the fight going against me, I had picked up a rock and threatened to throw it. The only way Mr. Benz could blunt the evidence was by making Combs admit that it had happened a long time ago when we were little kids.

My eighth-grade teacher, Miss Morrisson, was called to the stand, and she testified about the times I'd lost my temper, and how once I had

thrown a piece of chalk across the room in a fit of
anger.

But the most damaging testimony came
from Ted Feldman, who told how I'd jumped him
in the night, and how, beneath the moon high on
the bluff, I had wrestled him.

"He was like a madman," Feldman said.
"Jumped me from behind. Threw me to the
ground. Hit and kicked me. In fact, if I hadn't been
bigger and stronger, he might have killed me."

Mr. Benz was on his feet, objecting. "Pure
conjecture on the part of the witness. I ask the answer be struck."

"Objection sustained," the judge said.
"Strike that last response of Mr. Feldman's."

Then Mr. Benz turned to me and whispered, "————, boy, why didn't you tell me
about this so I could have been prepared for it?"

There was nothing I could say, or do, except
sink deeper and deeper into my chair. When the
district attorney had finished questioning Feldman,
Mr. Benz cleared his throat and asked:

"What were you doing up on the bluffs at
night?"

"Looking for Molly, for the dog. Matt
Tabor said if I found her, he would sell her to me."

"What made you think she might be up
among the bluffs?"

"I heard her baying, running coons."

178

"But you didn't find her."

"No, and I'll tell you why. Because Dan Stuart had been hiding her . . ." Mr. Benz started to object, but Feldman kept talking, "because he had been hiding her all along. Because he wanted that dog so bad he would kill to get her."

Mr. Benz took a quick, threatening step toward the witness. Feldman was quiet. "This is intolerable, Your Honor. May I request that the last be stricken and the witness be cautioned to answer only such questions as are asked."

"Strike the answer," the judge said, "and Mr. Feldman, we are not interested in what you think. We are only interested in your direct response to questions asked."

Mr. Benz came back to the table. He began to say something and then stopped. Obviously, he considered Feldman too dangerous a witness and that anything he said would only damage our cause further, so he said, "No more questions."

The prosecution rested its case with the testimony of Feldman. They had gotten everything in with a long list of witnesses. They had made me look like a hot-headed, irresponsible, impulsive boy capable of killing Tabor; they had put forward a motive and established that I was in the vicinity of where the crime was committed on the day it was committed. So, I thought, how can we refute them?

The judge adjourned court, and in the corridor, Mr. Benz just shook his head and said, "All we can hope for is sympathy. I don't see any other way."

Riding home was like riding to a funeral. No one spoke. After all, what was there to say. I had gotten a good look at a boy I had never dreamed existed.

Only when we turned into the yard did my father say, "It always looks worse than it really is just before it gets better. Tomorrow will be your turn. For every person who pictured you as something less than a good boy, we'll have a half dozen to refute his testimony."

I slept that night mainly, I suppose, because I was thoroughly exhausted. Never in my life, not even after falling down the bluff, had I felt so drained. In the morning, I was still tired. It was an effort just to get dressed.

It was Friday, and in court, Mr. Benz led a parade of character witnesses to the witness chair. There was the principal of my high school, the minister, several school teachers, a number of adult and younger friends . . . by noon my self-esteem had been somewhat patched up. Mr. Benz was doing what he said he would do. He was painting a picture for the women jurors of a good, kind boy caught up in a vicious web of circumstantial evidence.

180

He put on the stand the manager of the hardware store, who testified he'd sold hundreds of knives of the kind the D.A. had labeled as the murder weapon. Then he put on a laboratory technician who testified that he had examined the knife I now claimed was mine, and that the blood on it was that of an animal, and that it had been lying outside for weeks.

After lunch, he put me on the stand and let me tell my story in my own words—in my own way —and develop the theory that there were two identical knives involved, although, at first, I had thought the murder knife was mine.

My testimony took most of the afternoon. I felt good about being able at last to tell the story as it was; I even admitted to feeding Molly. I explained about everything. About how Jake Tabor had been careless with matches, how he had kicked Panther, and how I had not threatened him at all, but only said that someday *somebody* would kill him.

I accounted for my every move from the day Molly dropped out of sight until the day Tabor's body was found. I explained that I'd jumped Feldman because I thought he was the murderer. When I'd finished my story, it was beginning to get dark outside, and the judge adjourned the court until the following Monday.

181

18 All the testimony was in; now, an interminably long weekend stretched out ahead of us. Monday, Mr. Benz had explained, the D.A. would cross-examine me and he would present his summation to the judge. He warned that it would be a difficult time—that the district attorney would continue to picture me even more strongly as being capable of murder.

I knew that now. The prosecution had made a careful case. Feldman's testimony, his account of how I had perpetrated an unprovoked attack upon him, was the most dangerous. The district attorney was sure to argue that, if I was capable of a sneak attack in the dark on Feldman, I was capable of a sneak attack on Tabor—to kill him.

If I had only let Feldman pass. Or, instead of jumping him, if I had merely stepped out to identify him and then fled down the side of the bluff. To this day, I don't know why I leaped out on Feldman, except that—lying there in the brush —I had suddenly been convinced that there, stalking past me in the moonlight, was the real murderer, the man responsible for all my trouble. It must have been the medicine. Surely, no man or boy in his right mind would have been so foolhardy.

One thing I learned for certain. I was impulsive. I did do things on the spur of the moment, and without thinking them through to their logical conclusion. Why, otherwise, would I even have a desire to get out of bed—bruised as I was—and make a nighttime trip to the bluffs? Why, instead of bringing Molly and her pups in, did I hide them and feed them? Why the sudden anger when Tabor lighted matches in the barn? Why so many abrupt and, often, rash actions?

Mr. Benz had called it immaturity, but I was sure District Attorney Fessler would call it a vicious temper.

Saturday morning, after the chores, I stayed

in the barn. It was cold outside; but now that the cows stayed in the barn, it was warm, and a spider was spinning a web over a window pane through which the sun shone brightly.

It was peaceful in the barn. The rhythmic sound of cows chewing their cuds; the soft purring of the tiger cat as she rubbed against my leg; the soft thumping of Panther's tail every time he looked up into my face—all gave me a sense of calm.

Here, in the barn, there were no problems. The cattle were bred, and the calves came and grew up. All the cows asked was that they be fed, kept warm, and be relieved of their milk each morning and every evening.

Sitting there, I could sometimes hear the mice in the loose hay that the cows had pushed too far to be reached from their imprisoned positions in the stanchions. From far above, I could hear the quarreling of sparrows and the soft cooing of the pigeons that roosted in the cote attached to the haymow.

What a contrast, I thought, to the hectic excitement of Coulee City, to the almost electric intensity of the crowded courtroom. Right then and there, I vowed that if I retained my freedom, I would seek neither fame nor fortune, but be eternally grateful just to have a farm of my own where I could sit in the barn when the problems of daily living just seemed to be too much; to sit among the cattle—hear them move the hay about with their large, brown noses to find the most succulent twists and hear them sigh deeply when they found them.

The barn door at the far end rattled. I felt the cold draft sweeping in; when the door closed, I felt the warmth instantly close back around me. It was Dad. He came down the rows of brown cows and stopped in front of me.

"What about Molly?" he asked. "Has she got enough to eat?"

I had forgotten, for the time being, about Molly. There were too many other things to think about. "By now, she's probably out of food," I said.

"Then maybe you'd better take her some."

"Do you think I should try to bring her in?"

"Not now," Dad said. "Best to wait now until the trial is over."

"But what if . . ." I didn't finish the question, but my dad knew what I was thinking.

"Then you'll have to tell Matt Tabor where she is so he can go get her."

I expected my dad might sit with me and keep me company. Instead, he went up into the mow; shortly, I could hear him throwing down hay.

I got up, and Panther leaped to his feet. "Well, we'll take a walk," I said, and the dog pranced with delight.

In the feed shed, I fixed the straps to a fifty-pound bag of dog food so I could carry it on my shoulders with its weight resting against my back. I went to the house for a glass of milk; when I told my mother what I was going to do, she made me a sandwich.

The day was cold—even with the sun shining brightly—but with the fifty pounds on my back it wasn't long before I was sweating. Panther was exuberant. He barked at the junco flocks and chased my shadow. The snow had settled, and I walked without snowshoes. The walking was easy, and when I went past the Reims farm, I looked at the sheep all huddled in one corner of the pasture. I was glad Dad had suggested the food, or Molly would surely be back and walk into a trap or a shotgun blast.

When I got to the bluffs, I kept my eyes and ears open. I didn't want to run into Ted Feldman, or anyone, for that matter. All I wanted was to dump the food in front of the cave and get back home to the security, safety, and warmth of the barn and the house.

Going up the bluffs was more difficult than I had anticipated. The brief thaw had softened the snow; then, the sharp freeze had put a slick of ice on the steep incline. I moved upward from tree to tree, bush to bush, slowly and carefully.

It took me much longer than I had expected; by the time I got to the cave, Panther was already frolicking with the hound family.

The play stopped when the hounds smelled the food I was carrying; the pups clustered around me, almost tipping me over and back down the cliff. They must have been three months old, and they were at least three-fourths grown, each weighing perhaps thirty-five pounds.

I quickly slid out of the straps and, with my knife, slit open the bag. The pups dived in, getting mouthfuls of paper sacking in their eagerness to eat.

I stood back and looked at Molly. The red welts along her side where the buckshot had raked her had about healed, leaving long dark scars. Her eyes were sunken into her head, and her flews and her hide hung loosely from her thin body.

"Eat, Molly," I encouraged her, and then she moved slowly over to where the pups were glutting themselves and carefully, slowly, began to eat.

Panther stood off to one side and watched the pups gorge. I waited until, one by one, the pups flopped to the ground, their bellies distended, unable to eat another morsel. Almost half the fifty pounds had disappeared by the time they were sated. Then I turned and began the trek back.

The rest of the weekend went intolerably slowly. It wasn't until Sunday afternoon that the awful feeling of living in a void was broken—it took a blizzard to get the juices of living bubbling again.

The storm came out of the northeast with such suddenness and ferocity that all personal concerns were swept before it as we went out to keep paths open to the barn so we could feed the cattle; paths open to the pig sty where a sow was farrowing; paths open to the chicken house and the duck pen so feed could be scattered, ice dumped from the containers, and fresh water put down.

When the snow became too much for our shovels, we got out the tractor and, having no plow, mounted planks to the frame with which to push the snow from the drive, the entrance to the house, and away from in front of the barn door.

It was the kind of blizzard which could kill a man right in his own barnyard. Lights were indistinguishable at a distance of but a few feet. A man could get lost trying to get from the barn to the house and perhaps wander around until he collapsed and was covered with snow to die.

So, if it was a terrible inconvenience with tragic overtones for some, for us it was a godsend. We could forget about the trial in our fight to best the weather.

We even smiled as we came stomping into the entryway of the house to get hot coffee so we could go back out again to battle the cold and driving snow. The storm did not let up but howled across the fields until there were drifts almost as high as the corncrib—drifts up to the windows of

188

the house—until at last, instead of plowing a path to the pig sty, we tunneled.

It was something we could understand. It was something honest which we could fight. There was no pretense, no shadowboxing, no prevarication. It was a direct, head-on attack, and we could meet the storm on its most severe terms by fighting back with all our strength, with the best ideas our minds could come up with, with the roar of the tractor competing with the roar of the wind.

It was ten o'clock before the wind diminished and the snow stopped falling, and we were happily exhausted. The clouds drew back from the sky and the world glistened like a gigantic Christmas ornament.

Still we had to work—plowing, digging, stomping. The machine shed roof had to be shoveled clear lest it collapse. The sow with her new litter of eleven piglets had to be hog-tied and slid along the snow from the cold pig sty to a warm place in a calf pen in the barn. We were busy. Gloriously busy, and not once did we think of the trial, not once did we worry about tomorrow, because this night nature had come cracking down on us and we had gone right out to fight back.

By midnight, all was in order for the terrible cold which we knew almost always followed storms of such intensity. Then we all sat at the kitchen table sipping hot chocolate; even my two brothers

came sneaking down and were not sent to bed—
not until they, too, had their cups of hot chocolate.

Then, when we crept beneath the covers, we
slept, never dreaming, never coming sharply awake
in the dark—fearful of tomorrow—hardly moving
—victorious at least in this confrontation, which
we could understand, this fight which consumed all
our energies, all our skills.

In the morning, we awakened refreshed to
look out on a world so white and glistening that it
hurt our eyes. In the kitchen, I put my hand to the
frosted window and held it there until it had
melted a peep hole so I could look out at the ther-
mometer fastened to the sill. It had dropped to ten
degrees below zero.

"Extra rations for everybody today," my dad
said as we started for the barn to do chores. "Food
creates heat. It's one way of keeping our animals
warm."

I thought of Molly and wondered how she'd
fared. My dad must have known what I was thinking, because he said, "The dog will be all right.
She'll dig down to what food is left. You don't have
to worry about her. If snow brings cold, it brings
warmth, too. Piled up around their cave, it will act
as insulation."

When we opened the barn door, the cows
mooed as if glad to see us. Extremes of weather, it

seemed, made all farm animals apprehensive, as they must once have been many years before they were domesticated. What's more, they seemed to welcome the people who cared for them.

We were a little late, so we hurried. While the milking machines were rhythmically extracting milk from each cow's udder, we threw down twice the normal rations of hay. The hogs, the chickens . . . everything got double rations. Working out there—among the animals—the courthouse in Coulee City seemed a million miles away. So it was something of a shock to come up from the barn, slip out of my overalls and into a Sunday suit—only then did the fear come back . . .

My two brothers were also dressed and waiting when I came down. Since it was doubtful that the school bus would come by, it had been decided to let them spend the day with neighbors.

The apprehension I had felt on changing clothes quickly passed because all the way to town there was evidence of the storm's ferocity, and the gravity of it again became uppermost in our minds as we passed cars hopelessly buried in the ditches; miles of electric and telephone wires stripped from their poles and lost in the snow; trees, unable to carry their burdens, lying stricken, their bare branches thrusting out at grotesque angles.

Some smaller cottages were almost completely buried. We had to stop and back up several times to widenings in the narrow path the plow had left so approaching cars could get by. When we left my brothers off, they floundered up a drive that hadn't as yet been plowed.

In the city, people had to abandon the sidewalks to walk in the ruts left by cars. Signs were down. Here and there, a roof had caved in under the weight of snow. A storefront window had been demolished, and the furniture on display inside was covered with snow.

We made our way slowly, stopping sometimes to allow pedestrians to get out of the car ruts so we wouldn't run them down. When we came to the square where the courthouse stood, we had to drive around it several times while a jeep finished plowing out the parking lot. Only then could we edge the car up the drive, across the walk, and nose it up against the concrete curb which marked the boundaries of the parking lot.

Inside the courtroom, the storm and the devastation it had wrought was still felt. Though it was bright daylight, the ceiling lights were blazing; **19** in spite of the great difficulty in maneuvering in the snow-clogged streets, a large crowd had already claimed the spectator seats—their faces shone with the excitement the night had brought.

Court was to have convened at nine o'clock, but it was nine-thirty when we walked in. Mr. Benz left the long table to meet us and said the judge hadn't yet arrived.

"How'd you make out in the storm?" Mr. Benz asked my father.

"Fine. Just fine. No damage."

"What a blizzard! A real old-timer!" The attorney's eyes lighted up as he recounted how the wind had howled around his house until a door had been forced open and the snow had blown in through the front hall.

But here, in the courtroom, I couldn't feel the excitement of the storm. For me, there was only the smell of furniture polish, the smell of hot radiators, the odor of bodies, the murmur of spectators, the blue uniform of the bailiff, the white blouse of the court stenographer who sat so upright in her chair. Instead of the storm, it reminded me of the contest which would soon be shaping up inside this room, and I was wondering if I could weather it.

The judge didn't arrive until nearly ten o'clock, and then he joked about how he had to get his wife out to shovel so he'd have a path to the car. I wondered how he could be so light-hearted when this was the day my future would be decided.

For that matter, how could everyone—even Mr. Benz—smilingly make inconsequential conversation about such incredibly unimportant events as an electrical failure which had put his clock behind so he had almost overslept? Didn't these people know how I felt? This was the day on which a jury of eight men and four women would decide the entire future of my life.

Was it possible they didn't understand the

seriousness and the complete finality of being ad-
judged a murderer? How could they be so concerned about the depth of snow when the next five,
or ten, or twenty years of my life might be buried
in the time it took for twelve people to cast one
ballot?

Was all of life so unimportant that people
could watch a boy's future flushed away while all
they thought about was a pair of wet feet? A cold
nose? A frozen faucet?

It seemed incredible that people could be so
callous. How could the judge smile? How could
Mr. Benz and District Attorney Fessler inquire
about how the other had made it downtown? How
could the kids in the last row of spectator seats gig-
gle softly at some joke one or another had told?

I felt wretchedly abandoned. It wasn't important that I was fighting for everything that made
life worth living. It wasn't important that this
might be my last day of freedom.

I slumped lower into the chair. It didn't
make any difference that I was being tried for a
crime I hadn't committed. These people around
me weren't concerned that perhaps an innocent
boy might go to prison. All they could feel was a
strange sort of elation because the death which had
been riding the winds had passed them by, that
they had come through unscathed, that they had
been impervious to injury from the storm.

The smile left the judge's face when the jury

filed in. But I could even see the excitement of the storm on the jurors' faces although they had spent the night less than a block away locked safely in the Coulee City Hotel.

As soon as they were seated, I was called to the stand. At once, the storm seemed to be forgotten. Immediately, the old battle lines were drawn. The district attorney (who had only a moment ago been joking about how the snow had piled so high in front of his garage he had had to walk to the courthouse) began pacing in front of me, and I was reminded of an animal getting ready to spring.

It was hard to believe this was the same man I had thought to be a kindly man interested only in justice. When I had first seen him on the opening day of the trial, he had looked so calm and gentle; now, he stalked me—bent over almost in a crouch. Now his eloquent hands were hidden deep in the side pockets of his coat, and the lines of his face had deepened, which made him look predacious. His soft eyes had suddenly become piercing. His wavy, gray hair seemed fairly to bristle.

Yet, when he began questioning me, it was in a low, calculating, almost soft, voice, "You know you are still under oath . . . to tell the truth?" He made it a question.

I murmured, "Yes sir."

"Would you please speak up?" he asked.

"Yes sir," I repeated more loudly.

196

"That's better. Now you've told the jury that you were mending fence on the afternoon Jake Tabor was killed."

"That's right," I said.

"You told them you never saw Mr. Tabor on that afternoon."

"That's right. I didn't."

"Still, you went into the woods—into Black Haw Woods—to check on the dog. Isn't that true?"

"Yes, it's true."

"And Jake Tabor's body, when found, wasn't more than a few hundred yards from where the dog was hidden?"

"I believe that's right."

"And you mean to sit there and tell me that you could be so close to the scene of murder and still see nothing nor even hear an outcry?"

"I heard nothing."

"How is your hearing?" the district attorney asked. "How is your eyesight?"

"Good."

"Still, a man was killed within a few blocks of where you claim you were working and you never knew it?" The district attorney's voice, which had been calm and quiet, suddenly became explosive. The very impact of his voice, of his words on my senses, made me gulp. "Well?" the district attorney added.

"I didn't hear or see anything," I managed to say.

Suddenly, the animal who was the district attorney poised as though to make his killing. "And you know why?" he accused. "You know why you didn't hear or see anyone else kill Mr. Tabor?" He pointed a finger. "I'll tell you. It was because you were busy stalking him yourself. Because you were crawling through the woods, silently, behind Mr. Tabor. Because you were intent on murder. Because you were going to get your revenge. Then, when you were close enough, you leaped on his back—and you stabbed him, not once, but again, and again, and again. Isn't that true?" the district attorney said with a rapierlike thrust of words.

While the district attorney was raving each sentence, every word, cut into me like a sharp knife being thrust between a door and a door jamb to spring the lock. I could feel my stomach turn sour, feel my lungs ache for air, feel my head spin.

"Isn't that true!" the district attorney repeated, coming right down to within a few feet of me and hurling the accusation right into my face.

It was then all the tensions of the many weeks of waiting, worrying, bubbled up in me. It was at that precise moment that all the sleepless nights, the endless hours of watching as my mother faded, the fatigue, and the shame, and the torture of being wrongly accused came thrusting forward

198

like a flood of water pounding at a dam, and I exploded.

"No, it isn't true! You're making it up! You're a ——— liar! I never saw Jake Tabor! You're putting thoughts into the minds of the jurors which aren't true! You're not fair. You're not a good man!"

The judge was pounding with his gavel. The spectators were gripped by the drama of the moment, and there was an angry buzz in the courtroom. Mr. Benz had left his chair and came toward me, motioning with his hands for me to be quiet. The district attorney was leaning backward, grinning like the cat which had caught the mouse.

But even then, I didn't stop. "You're making it all up. You're evil! You don't even care about justice! All you want is to win this case!"

Although I didn't know it at the time, I was standing, leaning forward, holding a clenched fist out toward the district attorney, and I was shouting.

"It's men like you and Jake Tabor that make the world a terrible place to live! You're evil! You're bullies! Nothing but bullies!"

I didn't mean to, but I had taken a step toward the district attorney as though to attack him. There was bedlam in the courtroom. Spectators were standing. Some had come out into the aisles. Then I saw a blue uniform in front of me. The bailiff's arms closed around me, and he forced me back into the witness chair.

"That's enough," the bailiff was saying. "Sit down. Keep still! Stop it!"

I went limp then, slumped backward into the chair. The judge's gavel sounded above the frenzy of the crowd. But I was spent, burned out. Gradually, the courtroom quieted. Then it became so silent you could hear the snow squeak as cars went by on the street outside. When the district attorney came toward me, it was on tiptoe so as not to break the spell.

Then he said in a whisper, just loud enough for the judge and the jurors to hear, "I have no more questions. There need be no more questions. The defendant, I'm sure, has indicted himself."

I don't even know if Mr. Benz heard, because he didn't object. I doubt if anyone heard— anyone except me, and the judge, and the jurors. And I couldn't object, say anything, because I was as spent as the leaf which, after many battles with the wind, is finally torn from the tree.

When I went back to my seat, Mr. Benz said angrily, "Well, you really blew it. You really did." And I didn't care. I just didn't care. And at first, I didn't even hear the district attorney as he began his summation. But then, as he added up the evidence and I kept hearing my name, I was swept along again, helpless, on a torrent of evidence.

My thoughts must have been mirrored on my face because Mr. Benz whispered, "Buck up. Sit up straight."

I realized, of course, that the circumstantial evidence was considerable, but to hear it packaged the way the D.A. was packaging it, made it sound damning.

If I had thought his summation of the factual evidence was crushing, I was in no way prepared for the whiplashing he gave me once he had disposed of the evidence. He began counting up such individual characteristics as labeled me a headstrong, irresponsible, violent, somewhat stupid boy who was perfectly capable of killing without compunction.

I turned my head while he was talking to look to where my parents were seated in the first row. Tears were rolling down my mother's cheeks, and she made no effort to wipe them away. My father had his head hidden in his hands; I could see that his knuckles were white.

Mr. Benz put a hand to my shoulder as though to steady me; then, he tried to encourage me by whispering, "Maybe he'll overplay it. Maybe he'll ruin his own case. The jury knows you are not a scoundrel, that you are not stupid. His own eloquence may lose this case for him. There's going to be a backlash. It's too much."

But I was beyond taking hope from mere

words. I had heard so much about myself during the days in court that there were moments when I wondered who I really was, and what I really was, and how, overnight, I could have become such a despicable person.

Then the real explosion came. Like many explosions, it started slowly with what amounted to the sputtering of a fuse. The district attorney had finished his exhortation, had wiped his forehead with a white handkerchief, and the jurors, on the edges of their chairs, had eased back and looked relieved that he had finished.

Mr. Benz was shuffling papers on the long table as though that might help shuffle his thoughts, or line up as strong a case in my behalf as the district attorney had against me.

A deputy sheriff had come down the long aisle between the rows of spectators. He had opened the little, swinging gate and walked past our table straight to the bench. Standing there, his cap in hand, he handed the judge a folded piece of paper. The judge took it, adjusted his glasses, and then read.

Everyone was watching him. District Attorney Fessler, still standing in front of the jurors, had a frown on his face. Perhaps he felt the impact of his plea would be diluted by this diversion. Mr. Benz, his hand flat on the papers he had been shuffling, leaned forward as though crouched to

202

spring. The court reporter's mouth was open. She did not close it. The bailiff, who had stepped forward when the deputy approached the judge, stood with hands on hips, displaying consternation that the proceedings should have been disrupted.

Once, the judge looked up. Then abruptly, as if not believing what he had first read, he lowered his eyes to read again. His brow wrinkled, and there was a furrow between his eyes. Finally, he cleared his throat, picked up the gavel, and with a light tap on the desk, announced, "There will be a short recess."

Folding the paper, he got up and walked carefully down the three steps and, turning, went into his chambers. There was a buzz of excitement in the courtroom. District Attorney Fessler walked over to our table, and leaning toward Mr. Benz, whispered, "What's up?"

"Search me," Mr. Benz said.

I could hear people behind me moving restlessly. I saw the bewildered look on the face of the jurors. The sound of voices became more insistent now that there was no judge to keep order. Finally, I asked, "What do you think it is?"

Mr. Benz turned to me. "Probably nothing to do with our case."

I heard the double doors behind me swing open again, and then I heard steps. I turned. It was Sheriff Dobbie Stotz. His gun was slapping his thigh as he walked and he put a hand to the holster to hold it down. Without looking left or right, he went straight past the attorneys, past the bailiff, and, without knocking, went into the judge's chambers.

"Want a glass of water?" Mr. Benz asked. I nodded. He reached for the pitcher and poured me a glassful. It was lukewarm; it made me sick to my stomach. I looked back to where my parents were sitting. My mother was dry-eyed, and the ridge of muscle along my father's jaw was not jumping as spasmodically as it had been.

The sheriff stuck his head out of the judge's chambers and beckoned to the bailiff. When the bailiff went over to him, I heard him say, "Judge Hallock says to take the jurors out of the courtroom."

The bailiff went to the jury foreman and said, "We'll retire to the jury room for the time being." The jurors filed out. I turned around. None of the spectators had left. There was an air of expectancy. I got the feeling that something important was about to happen.

The sheriff came out of the judge's chambers and beckoned to the district attorney and Mr. Benz, who walked over and disappeared behind the massive, oaken door.

When fifteen minutes had passed and the door had not reopened, the spectators lapsed into silence. The noon hour came and the big hand of the clock began slowly to descend. Spectators began to move about on the benches. But they talked only in whispers.

Finally, the sheriff, his deputy, the district attorney, and Mr. Benz came out. Mr. Benz came directly to me and leaned over, whispering, "There's been a confession. Someone's confessed to the murder. But sit tight. Don't get your hopes too high."

I wondered who had confessed. And I also wondered, if there had been a confession, why Mr. Benz was not more jubilant about it. Why hadn't he come right out and told me that I was free, that I could go home, that they had the guilty party?

Instead, he had been cautious. He had said, "Don't get your hopes too high."

Finally, the jury came out and resumed their seats in the jury box. Judge Hallock came through the door and climbed back into his chair. He rapped once for order, and then called the district attorney and Mr. Benz to the bench. After a brief, whispered conversation, he announced: "There has been a disturbing development. Other evidence has presented itself. I cannot, however, discuss the nature of the evidence at this time. I do, instead, declare an indefinite recess." He tapped his gavel lightly once, got up, swept down the three steps as though angry, and disappeared into his chambers.

My parents came through the swinging gate

to the table. They approached me. "What's up?" my dad asked.

"There's been a confession."

"A confession!" my parents said simultaneously.

"Yes, a man has confessed to the killing."

"But who?"

"A Mr. Frazer."

My mother gasped. "Not Hugh Frazer?" she asked.

"That's right," Mr. Benz said. "Claimed he caught Tabor beating his dog and, in a moment of anger, killed him."

I looked at my mother. The back of her hand was pressed against her lips. Her eyes were wide with disbelief. "But he couldn't . . . he couldn't . . ." She checked herself. My father put an arm around her shoulders.

"Then why didn't the judge dismiss the charges against Danny?" my father asked.

"Because Sheriff Dobbie Stotz doesn't believe Frazer. He doesn't think Frazer did it."

"But then, why the confession?" my dad asked.

Mr. Benz shrugged. "Who knows. But, at least, it can't hurt us. I'll just have to find out more about Frazer."

I looked to my mother to see if she were going to volunteer any information. When I saw she wasn't, I wondered if I should.

"What happens now?" my father asked.

"Well, I suppose we can ask for a mistrial."

"What does that mean?" my father probed.

"It means that if Mr. Frazer's confession isn't bona fide—if it is a fabrication, for whatever reason—we may get a new trial, start all over. From the beginning."

Oh no, I thought. I couldn't. Not the long, torturous ordeal all over again. How could I stand it? How would my mother ever be able to stand it? It would be too much. I couldn't. I wouldn't.

"Well, you might as well go home. I'll keep you informed of any developments."

In the car, I tried to think about it. I could understand why the sheriff hadn't believed Frazer. Everyone knew he was a harmless old man. He was no man for murder. He was a gentle, kindly person. I think he even found it hard to kill the fish he caught.

I looked at my mother. Surely, she must have some thoughts on the matter. But she was tight-lipped and white, and then it struck me. It came to me all at once as a bright light suddenly illuminates a dark room.

Of course. He was doing it for her, for my mother, for his love for her all these many years. He was doing it for what probably was his first love, probably his only love, and at last, he had found a way in which he could show that love—by putting the rest of his life on the line for her son. It would be the perfect way for him to show her how deeply he had loved her.

I looked at my father, and I wondered if he had guessed. There was nothing showing on his face to indicate he had. But suppose he did know? My mother must have mentioned this affection Frazer had once shown toward her. It would only be natural for two people as close as my parents were to share everything in their past.

That night, it was on television, but Hughie's name was not mentioned. There was simply the announcement that the sheriff had said there were further developments in the Tabor murder case. He said that more evidence had come to light just as the case was to have gone to the jury.

I had nightmares all night. In the morning, I could tell by the look on my mother's face that she had slept poorly, too. After the breakfast dishes had been cleared away and my father was getting ready to go back outside, my mother turned to him. "I want you to take me to see Hughie," she said.

I expected my father to be surprised, but he wasn't. He only said, "Maybe they won't let you see him."

"We can try."

"Yes, we can try."

They started from the room to get ready. I followed, and said, "I want to go along. After all, it's me that all the trouble is about. I want to go along."

They both looked at me. Then my father said, "He's a man. He's a man now. He has a right to go along."

"But this is between Hughie and me," my mother protested.

"Not any longer," my father said. "Now it is between Hughie and all of us."

"He'll be embarrassed if we all show up."

"Maybe not."

"All right, then. But be kind."

For a moment, my father looked angry. My mother saw the look. "I'm sorry," she said. "I was only thinking of Hughie. I know you wouldn't hurt Hughie."

We changed clothes, drove to town, and stopped in front of the jail.

"But nobody's allowed to see Mr. Frazer," the desk sergeant said.

"Not even his attorney?" my father asked.

"He doesn't have one. He doesn't want one."

"Well, maybe that's what we want to talk to him about."

"Well, I don't know," the desk sergeant said, chewing on a pencil.

The jail door swung open and in with the cold came another deputy. He had Bob Bacon by the collar. The man had vomited on himself, and he was trembling uncontrollably. The desk sergeant leaned forward. "He doesn't belong here. He belongs in a hospital."

"I tried. The hospital wouldn't take him. They said they didn't have a bed."

"But he might die if you put him in a cell."

"Well, he's going to die for sure if I leave him out in the street."

Bacon had collapsed, was lying on the floor. My mother turned her head. I felt sick. The desk sergeant and the deputy tried to pick him up. His limp body slipped through their arms. My father stepped forward to help. They carried Bacon down the hall. Halfway to an open cell door, Bacon seemed galvanized into action. He writhed from their grasp, got to his feet, backed up against a wall —his eyes wide and haunted in his thin, bony face —and slurred:

"Matt did it! Matt Tabor did it! I saw him. I saw him kill his own father!"

My head snapped about. I saw my mother suddenly looking at Bacon with an incredulous look. The three men who had been closing in on him stopped. Bacon screamed again, "Tabor did it. Matt killed his father. But he deserved to be killed. I'm glad Matt killed him. I'm glad he killed him."

Bacon collapsed unconscious to the floor. "Get a doctor," the desk sergeant said to the deputy. "Get a doctor."

210

Epilogue

When we got home late that night, I couldn't sleep. I got up, dressed, and trudged through the snow into the barn. I thought . . . in this uncomplicated place . . . perhaps I could sort out my thoughts.

Matt Tabor had come forward and confessed, and although I was very relieved to say the least, I somehow didn't feel jubilant. I felt a great sadness, and it had nothing to do with my ordeal; with the predicament of Molly and her pups, the bestiality of the dead man, or even with the tragic consequences of Matt Tabor's or Bob Bacon's misdeeds.

Instead I thought about Hughie (Big Fish)

211

Frazer. I thought about his one-room shack where for more years than I'd been alive, he'd perhaps nurtured a love which could not be. As I sat there smelling the hay and listening to the deep breathing of the warm cows, Hughie's life story gave me a sudden feeling of tremendous strength. Here was a gentle man—certainly no man for murder—whose love had been so strong and so enduring that he was willing to sacrifice all those years yet left to him to keep me out of prison, because it would have made my mother happy.

The cow I was sitting beside moved, got up. I jumped so as not to be stepped on. A tiny breeze from the movement of both our bodies trembled the dust covered web a spider had spun across a window pane. Moonlight, splintered by the web, trembled on the barn floor.

MEL ELLIS

Born and raised in central Wisconsin, a graduate of the University of Notre Dame, Mel Ellis has always been an outdoorsman, fishing and hunting all over America. A former outdoor editor of the *Milwaukee Journal*, he is also the author of several hundred articles published in such well-known magazines as *National Geographic* and *True*. From his knowledge of wildlife and conservation has come the inspiration for many of his works, including: SAD SONG OF THE COYOTE; SOFTLY ROARS THE LION; IRONHEAD; WILD GOOSE, BROTHER GOOSE; RUN, RAINEY, RUN; CARIBOU CROSSING and THIS MYSTERIOUS RIVER. Mr. Ellis presently resides with his wife and family on fifteen acres in Wisconsin.